THE PRINCE

Tim Richards

ALLEN & UNWIN

Also by Tim Richards

Letters to Francesca

First published in 1997 by
Allen & Unwin Pty Ltd
9 Atchison Street, St Leonards, NSW 2065 Australia
Phone: (61 2) 9901 4088
Fax: (61 2) 9906 2218
E-mail: frontdesk@allen-unwin.com.au
URL: http://www.allen-unwin.com.au

National Library of Australia
Cataloguing-in-Publication entry:

Richards, Tim, 1960– .
    The prince.

    ISBN 1 86448 285 0.

    I. Title.

A823.3

Set in 11/13pt Caslon 540; 10/12pt Times; 10/12pt Memorandum;
11/13pt Caslon 224 by DOCUPRO, Sydney
Printed by Australian Print Group, Maryborough, Victoria

10 9 8 7 6 5 4 3 2 1

THE PRINCE

edited by Thomas Dixon

INTRODUCTION

Is it possible to locate an Australian who doesn't hold an opinion about the Hampton Festival of Killing? Only the Kelly Gang's siege at Glenrowan, and the mysterious disappearance of Azaria Chamberlain at Uluru come close to challenging Hampton's Festival for notoriety.

The six years since the collapse of the Festival have seen the publication of seventeen books, two stage dramatisations, an opera, five feature films, three feature-length documentaries, two cartoon series, and a television quiz show. At the time this volume went to press, two further films were in production, one to be shot in a Scottish village, and the other, *Backwater*, to be filmed in the town of Eden on the New South Wales coast.

As time passes, the Hampton myth feeds off itself and takes on a narrative life of its own. Following a pattern established by the Hollywood western, film-makers and authors have tended to use previous films and fictions about Hampton's Killer as source materials. The facts of the case become ever murkier. The 195 cm tall Swede, Daniel Lundquist, set a trend for the casting of tall athletic blondes to play Richard Thompson. Now we are shocked to see footage of the real Killer, just 170 cm tall with wavy dark hair, and seldom dressed so suavely as those who depict him on screen. We are shocked also to be reminded that 'the real Thompson' (a dangerous presumption, if ever there was one) never used a gun or a knife to dispose of his fellow Hamptonians. Screenwriters versed in the lore of the cinema apparently find it impossible to imagine a Killer who did not employ the screen killer's standard weaponry.

And producers seem unable to resist the temptation of devising a passionate love-interest for the Killer. Yet the one aspect of Thompson's personality that most fascinates scholars is his 'ability' to resist sexual temptation, while remaining conscious of that temptation. In his journal, the Killer refers to this semi-voluntary celibacy as his 'weird priesthood'.

Under the sway of post-Jungian theorists like Joseph Campbell, many scholars are determined to construct a version of Thompson that readily obeys classical heroic models: Hampton's Killer must be either hero or anti-hero, seldom if ever a combination of both. His many complexities, contradictions and personal confusions are smoothed over to facilitate the creation of an easy-to-digest moral fable.

Sides must be taken.

Lately it has become the accepted wisdom to deride Hampton's Festival of Killing as a barbarous social experiment or mad folly. Many historians have been keen to bracket Hampton with the former Soviet Union, and to view the Festival's ultimate failure as inevitable—a failure to recognise and accept the constants of human nature. Yet complacent 20/20 hindsight only serves to obscure the discoveries still to be made through close analysis of Hampton's unique contract of association. The anthropologist Gabriella Rossi has gone so far as to suggest that the final demise of the Hampton Festival represents not the triumph of decency and common sense over evil, but the death of romantic vision at the hands of cynical opportunism.

My first-hand knowledge of the Killer is slight. I met Richard Thompson just once, when I was a member of an academic delegation that visited Hampton to protest the depravity of the Festival. Thompson listened carefully to our arguments but refused to debate them. Later, he sent me a short note.

> I understand your views, but I cannot respect them. You are seeking to condemn the culture of my tribe without having sought to understand the specific circumstances and imperatives which gave rise to that culture. You condemn the citizens of Hampton on the basis of universal terms that simply do not apply.*

It is not my intention in this volume to rehearse arguments related to the morality or utility of the ideas which produced the Festival. Nor is this the occasion to rehash the legal questions related to accusations of criminality made against Hampton's Killer. Those matters, and matters related to the alleged conspiracy to implicate Richard Thompson, have been dealt with at great length in my previous books, *The Loaded Mirror* and *A Model Society*.

My hope is that this slim volume will offer a new source of primary materials to enable a more considered, scholarly analysis of Hampton's Festival. Following the judgement of the Witherspoon Commission, it is now possible to publish in full the hitherto suppressed 'October' segment of Richard Thompson's personal journal. These journal entries offer a fascinating insight into the Killer's notoriously enigmatic personality, and the circumstances leading up to the Festival's demise. By publishing the crucial journal entries alongside Christine Marker's

---

* Honesty compels me to report that Thompson made brief reference to this delegation in his journal, wherein he chose to describe me as 'a snivelling, morally superior shithead'. See *If Looks Could Kill: The Diaries of Richard Thompson*, edited by Miranda Murray.

Channel 4 transcripts, the two letters of disputed origin, and a newly discovered letter written by Christine Marker to her sister, we may now find it possible to piece together a more complete picture of the most curious social experiment in Australia's history.

I am particularly indebted to my colleague and partner Miranda Murray for her assistance in indexing the small mountain of testimony and documentary evidence presented before the original coronial inquest, and the subsequent Elliot and Witherspoon Commissions. It is to her that I humbly dedicate this book.

Thomas Dixon
Professor of Australian Studies
Calwell University

PART 1

TRANSCRIPTS TO
THE SOCIAL CONTRACT

The physical makeup of man is the handiwork of nature: the constitution of the State is the product of art. *It is not in men's power to prolong their lives, but they can prolong the life of the State for as long as possible by devising the best possible form.*

—The Social Contract, *Jean-Jacques Rousseau, 1762*

. . . that the object of mans desire is not to enjoy once onely, and for one instant of time; but to assure for ever, the way of his future desire. And therefore the voluntary actions, and inclinations of all men, tend, not onely to the procuring, but also to the assuring of a contented life; and differ onely in the way; which ariseth partly from the diversity of passions, in divers men; and partly from the difference in the knowledge, or opinion each one has of the causes which produce the effect desired . . .

—Leviathan, *Thomas Hobbes, 1651*

Midway through July in the fifth year of Hampton's Festival, the renowned Anglo-French film-maker Christine Marker was commissioned to make a feature-length documentary on the Hampton Festival of Killing. At that stage, the Festival had already claimed thirty-two lives. Financed by Britain's Channel 4 in partnership with Amnesty International, Marker's film was intended to be the first documentary examination of the Festival to be made with the participation of Hampton Council.

Marker and her three-person crew (Michael Tynan on camera, Penny Donaldson on sound, and the researcher–production assistant Gillian Chatterton) arrived in Hampton in early October. During the next month, they taped thirty-nine interviews. Many of these interviews are preserved in the transcripts Christine Marker sent to Michael Ambrose, her Executive Producer in London, after Hampton police seized her videotapes.

Apart from comments made in letters written by the film-crew, journal entries made by Richard Thompson, and the testimony of several interviewees, the transcripts are all that remain of the documentary that Marker proposed to call *The Social Contract*. The audiotapes, notebooks and diaries to which Marker refers in her correspondence vanished, and are presumed destroyed.

The authenticity of the Marker transcripts remained a matter of legal dispute until the Witherspoon Commission overturned a ruling made by the previous Elliot Commission. Justice Witherspoon accepted that the documents were a complete and authentic representation of a correspondence sent by Christine Marker to Michael Ambrose on November 11. Following this determination, Justice Witherspoon withdrew the order which had suppressed publication of the transcripts.

Christine Marker
Passchendaele Hilton
Hampton
November 10

Michael Ambrose
Executive Producer
Channel 4 Films
LONDON

Dear Michael,

As you'll be aware from the faxes sent to Sarah, things have taken a dramatic turn in the past few days, and the immediate future of the Festival is uncertain.

On Thursday, Richard Thompson failed to appear for an interview with the Head of Internal Security, and a warrant was issued for his arrest.

At about the same time, a dozen police arrived at our hotel, ransacked our rooms, and confiscated my videotapes, computer and discs. They told us that they had reason to believe that the tapes held information pertaining to the murder of Keiko Morimoto. We had interviewed Morimoto in the week prior to her murder. Though the Mayor and the Head of Internal Security have given an undertaking that the tapes and discs will be returned once they have been copied, they will give no indication when this duplication will take place. I am extremely concerned that the Council won't honour these assurances, and I urge you to make a representation to them on our behalf, preferably under an Amnesty International letterhead.

In the meantime, Gill has reconstructed most of the interviews from our unseized audiotapes and continuity notes. I think it best that you hold a copy of these transcripts in case we are subjected to further confiscations and interrogation. The local legal system is highly idiosyncratic. I am particularly worried that material in the confiscated tapes might be used to compromise interviewees to whom we promised confidentiality.

Before the Morimoto tragedy, it seemed likely that the final killing of the year would take place sometime in early December. At the moment, I doubt whether Richard Thompson would be permitted to

4

continue in his role as the Killer, and whether he would wish to execute the seventh killing of the year, even if permitted. Thompson is a genuine enigma. He impresses as being at the same time forthright and deceptive. I couldn't even offer an educated opinion about his possible involvement in Morimoto's murder.

I am sure that you will accept the necessity for us to stay on through the resolution of the current crisis. I'll fax through a revised budget in the next couple of days.

In the meantime, I would be very appreciative if you would seek the assistance of the Foreign Office to gain the speedy return of the tapes and computer. If the police refuse to return the tapes, we will require legal assistance. I believe Sarah has the originals of the contracts we entered with Hampton Council.

These transcripts represent a third to a half of the material that we've shot, and I am very confident of the quality of the footage we have. I'll keep you informed of further developments.

Yours

Christine

Christine Marker

1. Richard Thompson, Killer—October 17

We filmed the Killer in an arranged interview at his unpretentious Fewster Road home, tracking through the front door past a security guard. Richard Thompson is a conservatively dressed, friendly man in his early thirties. We see him surrounded by bookcases full of paperback novels, biographies, philosophical works, and film criticism. On one wall, there is a framed Kandinsky (possibly an original), 'Street Scene in Murnau'. Beneath this is a framed photograph, 'Hampton Street, in the vicinity of Hampton Station, 1913'. Though he seemed to be geared for criticism, Thompson remained calm, and sipped coffee throughout the interview.

When did you decide that you'd become Hampton's Killer?

THOMPSON: It was a combination of circumstances, really . . . I was coming back to live in Hampton, and I needed work. The Council wanted a Hampton person who cared about the future of Hampton . . . I grew up here, went to the local schools, church, scouts, that sort of thing.

You were a teacher?

THOMPSON: Yes, I taught English and Media studies at high school.

A good teacher?

THOMPSON: Not particularly. I liked aspects of teaching, working with the texts, seeing kids charged with new ideas or ways of thinking, but that didn't happen all that often. I wasn't good with the uncommitted kids, the kids that were filling in time. It disappointed me that so much of teaching was delimitation and control . . .

Like killing?

THOMPSON: A different sort of thing. With students, you have to restate and redefine roles and relationships.

Here, people know what the Killer's role is. They accept that I have a certain job to do.

That you are a professional killer . . .

THOMPSON: That I'm paid to kill seven people a year.

How many people have you killed?

THOMPSON: Thirty-three. This is the fifth year of the Festival.

Are you proud?

THOMPSON: Pride is a loaded term. I'm not sure that it's the word that I'd use . . .

But you enjoy killing?

THOMPSON: There are two aspects to each kill. First, there's the planning and execution. I don't think that anyone could say that they enjoy the kill. It's very solemn. You're trying to combine decency with efficiency . . . It needs to be orderly, and you want to be sure in your own mind that they understand and accept why you're killing them.

They? . . . The victim?

THOMPSON: Yes. You have to do things properly.

And the second aspect?

THOMPSON: Afterwards. When people seek you out in the street. The respect and celebrity that they give you. The Killer is the lifeblood of this community, someone special. And as the Festival draws nearer, there's a momentum, a tremendous anticipation that you're at the centre of.

Because you kill human beings . . .

THOMPSON: Because I perform an essential social function that binds this community together, that allows Hampton to be prosperous, and to share its prosperity . . . Before the Council ran with the Festival concept, Hampton was finished. Businesses were closing, churches were being pulled down, the high school was demolished, there wasn't even any sand on the beach . . . You can't be a beach suburb without sand. The Festival gives Hampton a face, an identity. It allows Hampton to continue to be Hampton.

But, in the final analysis, it's all about money?

THOMPSON: No, community is what it's all about. The prosperity comes from the strength and single-mindedness of the Hampton community. The Killer is the embodiment of that single-mindedness, and Hampton's prosperity is a bi-product of our success in shaping a genuine community.

2. Lorraine di Stasio, Hampton Mayor—October 19

The slightly cross-eyed Lorraine has been on the Hampton Council for nine years. She was instrumental in Hampton's successful campaign to gain the status of an Independent Territory, and this is her second term as Mayor. She is an enthusiastic woman in her mid-fifties. We see her seated in the Council chambers, dressed in her mayoral robes.

How did the Festival of Killing come about?

LORRAINE: The idea was first proposed seven or eight years ago. At the time, people said that it was outrageous. How could you sanction someone to kill seven residents each year? But Hampton was practically dead then. The businesses in the local shopping strip were being killed off by the massive shopping malls in nearby suburbs. The Victorian Government treated Hampton like a poor relation. We'd lost our school, our beach. There would have been nothing left of Hampton's character if we hadn't acted. State Government ministers were telling us that we should turn the suburb into exclusive golf courses for Japanese businessmen. So we formed a breakaway Council, with sub-committees investigating a variety of financial strategies . . . The Festival idea kept re-emerging, but there are so many festivals: arts festivals, comedy festivals, food festivals, sporting carnivals. Our festival had to be something unique, something that would make Hampton a centre of national focus.

Now Hampton is internationally notorious . . .

LORRAINE: Yes, because we tapped into something that really interests people.

Murder.

LORRAINE: Not murder, killing. It's a Festival of Killing. When you say murder, it implies that something's

9

done against a person's will. We were able to say to our people, Look, we have a strategy that will make Hampton the most comfortable, desirable suburb in Melbourne, something that will breathe life back into the place. To do that, we need to hire someone to kill seven residents each year, no more, no less. The killings will be at random. No one has to stay, but if you want to run a business in Hampton, you'll need to be a permanent resident of Hampton. When the seventh killing takes place, we'll hold a week of festivities, a big, emotional thanksgiving. We said to the Hampton people, If you let us stage this Festival of Killing, we can save Hampton from dying . . . At the beginning, I'm sure that no one anticipated just how big the Festival would become. A lot of people left, thirty per cent of the population, but now people are voting with their feet. Real estate in Hampton has gone through the roof. The Federal Government granted us Independent Territorial status. We're like an island within metropolitan Melbourne, and Hampton has community facilities that are unmatched by any community anywhere. The Festival has enabled us to build the finest art gallery in the southern hemisphere, and we expect that within ten years it will be the finest gallery of modern art in the world. There's a holiday atmosphere here all year round, and the Festival itself is a joy beyond our wildest imaginings.

But how do you reckon the price of a human life?

LORRAINE: How do you measure the worth of genuine community? Hampton people are bound together by this great adventure, they're successful, they know that anything worth accomplishing involves sacrifice.

Thirty-three lives so far . . .

LORRAINE: People that died willingly, people that died happy in the knowledge that they've left joy, gratitude,

10

and prosperity behind them . . . You've seen our
Shrine of The Martyrs?

Yes.

LORRAINE: It's very beautiful. It's very tasteful. The
Shrine's one of Hampton's most popular attractions.

3. Wendy Billingsley, Hampton Tourist Commissioner—October 20

Wendy is a young tyro who has lived in Hampton all her life. We filmed her at the Hampton Tourist Authority, in a luxurious office which overlooks both the bay, and the Shrine of The Martyrs. Her office is part of a recently constructed twenty-storey complex on Hampton Street which is also a set-down point for tourist buses.

What is the Festival worth to the local community?

WENDY: It's difficult to say exactly. Hampton has something like 15 000 residents. Festival Week itself will bring more than 300 000 people into Hampton. There has been an estimate that the all-round income generated from the Festival this year will be something in the order of thirty billion dollars. On average, we get fifty tour buses through every day of the year, to see the Shrine, to see the statue of the Killer. Of course, everyone wants to see the Killer in the flesh. The hotel where your crew is staying used to be an Italian restaurant, now it's a five-star international hotel with four hundred rooms which overlook Hampton and the bay. We have new industries setting up . . . You've seen The Killer's Beer. All the merchandising is quite phenomenal. T-shirts, maps of the killing sites, project posters of the weapons used, photo-montages of the victims, board games, mugs, video-games, swap cards. Then there's the betting . . . Just five years ago, ninety per cent of Hampton people worked outside Hampton. Now you'll find that the vast majority of them derive their income from Festival-related business, even if it's only renting out a bungalow in the weeks leading up to the seventh killing.

So the Festival's gradually become more than just one week of the year?

WENDY: That's the whole beauty of having seven killings. It's something that we never anticipated. We've found that a whole series of 'mini-events' have self-generated around each killing. Of course, you've got the funerals, and a week of mourning . . . The first killing of the new year has taken on a special significance. It's become known as the Profanity. There's a very solemn parade where the community celebrates the importance of the undertaking that binds them. It's now traditional for the Killer to remain out of public view for the week following the Profanity. We even refuse to allow an official betting market on the date of the Profanity . . . Like I said, there's a special parade, and the Killer's effigy is burnt on the steps of the Shrine of The Martyrs. But after that, each killing brings a rising level of anticipation and excitement. The gambling begins to escalate . . . It's fantastic!

What about Richard Thompson?

WENDY: Another of our traditions is that the Killer is never referred to by his given name. It's out of deference to his public responsibility.

Could another person become the Killer?

WENDY: Sure. The Killer operates according to yearly contracts, but this Killer's been fantastic for Hampton. He's a very intelligent, thoughtful man. He's terrific with the media. Some people think that all he has to do is knock-off seven residents each year—Actually, that **is** all he's required to do according to the terms of his contract. He could be totally reclusive if he chose to be. But the Killer's very civic-minded. He deals with the press, with international television. He gave one thousand interviews last year. He speaks to tour groups, he appears at non-Festival functions. He loves Hampton, and the Hampton people have a reciprocal feeling for him. The most important event of the Festival Week is the Killer's Parade, when he's

13

driven down Hampton Street on the back of a massive
float, being kissed and hugged by the families of that
year's Martyrs, being cheered and showered with rose
petals. It's tremendously moving.

So what is happening in Hampton now?

WENDY: Well, we're waiting for the sixth killing. Once
that's taken place, we can start putting up the billboards and the banners, organising the floats. The
long-term tourists come in, to wait for the last killing. Sometimes that can be ten or twelve weeks. All
the time the atmosphere is building up. The tension's
enormous. It's a sensational time.

You've lost a brother?

WENDY: Yes . . . In the third year.

**He used to work with you here at the Tourist Author-
ity?**

WENDY: Johnny was terrific. I miss him so much.
Everyone does . . . Cyanide poisoning. It was very
quick.

A shame.

WENDY: It's exactly how he would've wanted it.

4. Doug & Mavis Shrimpton, The Killer's Neighbours—October 20

We filmed the elderly Shrimptons in their front garden, which overlooks the Killer's own front garden. One of his security guards wanders in and out of shot in the background.

MAVIS: When we heard that the Killer would be moving in next door, well, naturally we were very apprehensive. I mean, we knew Richard from when he used to live in Hampton as a schoolboy. He was a sweet, quiet boy, but he wasn't a killer then. You don't know how being a killer might change someone, the sort of people he might associate with.

DOUG: He used to play cricket with our Joe . . .

So you knew before he arrived that your neighbour would be the Killer?

MAVIS: Yes. The Council bought the house specifically to be the Killer's residence. That's why it's so well maintained.

DOUG: The security's something terrific . . .

MAVIS: Of course, we asked for assurances.

Assurances?

MAVIS: That he wouldn't be doing the killing next door. As you know, he uses a lot of different methods: electrocution, injections, crossbows . . . We're told that it's quick and clinical, but it's not the kind of thing that you want happening over the side fence.

DOUG: Not on any regular basis.

MAVIS: There would have been police and ambulances coming at all hours of the night.

DOUG: The Council assured us that the Killer wouldn't be bringing his business home.

What kind of neighbour is he?

DOUG: Friendly. He'll always smile and speak if he sees you in the street. But he's quiet. Keeps very much to himself.

Girlfriends?

MAVIS: Not as such . . . Not that we know of. You see quite a few girls drop by, their mothers send them by with cakes and casseroles and things. I suppose that they might have, what do you call them . . .?

DOUG: Ulterior motives.

MAVIS: Well, he's a very sensible lad. I don't see him being swayed by something like that.

You're not bothered that your neighbour might decide to kill one or both of you?

DOUG: Not in the slightest. It'd be an honour. When you think of the good he's done for Hampton.

MAVIS: Of course, he wouldn't be allowed to kill the two of us at once, not since the Nguyens a couple of years back. That got the bookmakers in a helluva flap, wanting to know who went first, was it the man or the woman? Then, Mr Nguyen was over thirty-five, and she was under. It upset all their betting categories, so the Council changed the regulations so that the sequence of deaths had to be separated by at least the one week of mourning.

DOUG: Did we tell you that he painted our letterbox?

5. Nick Ptsouris, Chief Inspector, Hampton Police—October 23

We filmed Inspector Ptsouris sitting on the bonnet of a police divisional van parked in the street. He waved and smiled as pedestrians went past. At one point, a small group of Korean tourists stopped to photograph the interview.

How do you find out about each killing?

NICK: The Killer has a special hotline. He contacts us immediately after each kill. There are code words, that sort of thing.

Does he meet you at the scene?

NICK: No, there's a protocol. The Killer leaves the scene before we arrive. Then our responsibility is to determine what happened independent of any input from the Killer.

Why can't he just tell you what he's done, and how he did it?

NICK: There's the danger that he might accidentally reveal some part of his methodology—why he chose a certain person or mode of killing—and then his position would be compromised.

But isn't his position already compromised by everyone knowing who the Killer is?

NICK: When the Festival idea first came up, the suggestion was put that the Killer should be anonymous . . . But then we reckoned that we'd have amateur Columbos coming in from all over, prying into everyone's lives, as if Hampton was a giant Cluedo board. Another suggestion was that there should be a Kill Roster, that each citizen would be rostered to kill a person whose name was pulled out of a barrel at a designated time, but that mitigated against efficiency. Not everyone has the skill to be an efficient killer, and you don't want victims wandering through the streets with a crossbow bolt through their cheek,

17

y'know, bleeding to death . . . Finally, it was accepted that the Killer would have to be someone widely recognised, someone who could be celebrated for doing a difficult job for the Hampton community. We don't think of the Killer as an ordinary citizen, we see him as the embodiment of the community's will.

So the police have no idea of who he'll kill or when?

NICK: No idea.

It could be you.

NICK: Yes, it could.

Have you formed any theories on how he decides on the next victim?

NICK: Everyone has theories—Names out of a hat, or some convoluted sociological distribution . . .

But there's no way to ensure that his method is perfectly random, that some kind of favouritism won't come into it. The Killer would be very open to corrupt approaches.

NICK: Absolutely. That's where it becomes an act of faith.

Faith?

NICK: Yes, I think so. Trust.

But there have been complaints, haven't there?

NICK: Of course. I mean, it's only natural that in the week after your wife, or father's been killed, a relative's going to complain that it's unfair, or too calculated. No one in Hampton has tried to legislate against grief. But people do come around. Finally, they accept that the killing allows us to survive and prosper as a society.

Do Richard Thompson's friends and family prosper?

NICK: It was agreed that they should leave Hampton prior to the first killing.

But he'd make new friends, be attracted to young women, offered entreaties . . . I've heard it said that some mothers have sent their young daughters to seduce him . . .

NICK: I've heard it said that he's a homosexual . . . If you listen long enough, you'll hear every sort of rumour. The place is rife with gamblers and their gossip . . . Look, you'd have to ask the Killer about entreaties. We're satisfied that there's been nothing improper about the killings.

Nothing? . . . What about Angela Kaufmann?

NICK: What about her?

She was fifteen years old. There were allegations that she'd been interfered with before the killing . . .

NICK: (VERY ANGRY) That's ridiculous! I attended that scene. Who makes those allegations? None of those allegations ever come from within Hampton. Outside people get very niggly about our wealth. We live well, very well, in a close community, our kids are well clothed and well educated . . . Envy is a terrible thing. Outsiders resent the sacrifices that Hampton people have made, and they try to undermine the success of the Festival. I've heard every sort of lie. But the proof of the pudding is that right across Europe and Asia and America, you have small towns trying to emulate the Hampton experience.

So Angela Kaufmann wasn't raped?

NICK: No. She was not interfered with in any way.

Would it have made any difference if she had been raped before she was killed?

NICK: Don't be ridiculous! What do you take us for? We could never condone that sort of thing. If you're going to make allegations, let's see some proof to substantiate them.

6. Richard Thompson, Killer—Public Park, October 23

<u>On this occasion we filmed Thompson in a small park while he gave a public demonstration of target shooting with a crossbow. Three security guards held back a large crowd of tourists and locals who applauded each accurate shot. We questioned Thompson while he was reloading.</u>

Can you tell us about the Angela Kaufmann killing?

THOMPSON: Sure, that was two seasons back. I met her as she was on the way home from school.

Was she with friends?

THOMPSON: No, the killings have to be much more discreet than that. You'd have a betting plunge if I was seen escorting someone away from a group.

What happened?

THOMPSON: I told Angie that I was going to kill her, and that it would be best if we did it at her place. She was very calm about it. In fact, I remember her asking me if I was nervous. She also wanted to know if she'd have time to write any letters.

Did you let her write the letters?

THOMPSON: One, I think. I remember that it was a very finely balanced kill time-wise. You can't afford to have other people on the scene distracting you. I figured that I had about ninety minutes before her parents got home. Generally, I like to make a kill, get off the scene, notify the police, and have the police waiting when the victim's next of kin arrive. It would be too horrible if family had to discover the body.

Did you find Angela attractive?

THOMPSON: Look, don't think that I don't know what you're getting at . . . Angie was a terrific kid. I had a job to do. She accepted that.

Did you find her attractive?

THOMPSON: She was a pretty girl.

You smothered her with a pillow.

THOMPSON: You'll find all that in the police report.

She was dressed in her nightie . . .

THOMPSON: That's untrue. She was dressed in a windcheater and jeans. Check the report.

But you've heard the allegations that have been made?

THOMPSON: I suppose that I should take it that you're repeating them? **(LONG PAUSE)** They're fictions. I hear all sorts of insinuations and sleazy innuendo. I've been spat on by outsiders. All that goes with the job. It's no rose garden. But you won't find the Kaufmann family making any accusations. I can look Angie's family in the eye . . . Speak to them yourself. They know that I treated their daughter with care and decency.

You smothered her to death.

THOMPSON: I gave Angie the choice of being electrocuted, injected or smothered. Sometimes, when a kill has to be really quick, I'm not able to offer a choice.

How do you choose an intended victim?

THOMPSON: I have a random method . . .

What is that method?

THOMPSON: I can't divulge it.

You don't try to choose 'the deserving'?

THOMPSON: Never. It's not my business to make moral judgements.

You don't play at being God?

THOMPSON: No. I kill seven people a year.

Do you believe in God?

THOMPSON: Well, I believe that God would probably do a better job than me if He or She was contracted to be Hampton's Killer, but, things being what they are, and the community's expectations being what they are, I do a pretty fair job.

Do you have a killing schedule?

THOMPSON: Sometimes I decide a month in advance, sometimes I decide an hour or two before I make a kill . . . It comes down to a judgement about when it will be most efficient.

Does it get messy?

THOMPSON: It can. I guarantee a quick kill, but that doesn't always mean it will be a clean kill.

You once made a claim on the Council for a new pair of shoes . . .

THOMPSON: Yes, they were saturated in blood. You shouldn't imagine that it's an easy thing being a killer.

But you are so well paid. Don't you think that it was insensitive? You killed a mother of six, and then you hit the Council for the cost of new shoes . . .

THOMPSON: Yeah, well that's not how it happened. There was a lot of blood at the scene. The police found my footprints everywhere . . . The police thought that it would be better for them if I didn't track blood all through Hampton. When they took the shoes, they suggested that I should claim for them. The Council also cleans my car and carpets from time to time. But you're right. I do make a lot of money from performing my duties as Hampton's Killer. And I am aware of the need to be sensitive. You'll notice that I drive a rusty twenty-year-old Datsun. All of my investments are channelled back into Hampton companies.

Do you believe that it's wrong to kill your fellow human beings?

THOMPSON: That's a big moral question . . . I'm not sure that I have the time.

When will you have the time?

Just at that moment Thompson was besieged by kids looking for autographs.

When will you have the time?

THOMPSON: I'm giving a public lecture about the morality of killing next Thursday . . . You'll have to get the Council's permission to film.

BOY: (CHEEKY) Hey, can you autograph my bum?
THOMPSON: (FRIENDLY) How would you like me to kill your mother and eat her?

7. American Tourists at Killer Mural—October 26

<u>We filmed a group of mostly elderly Americans posing in front of the large mural portrait of Thompson engaged in various acts of killing, on the outer wall of Hampton Primary School.</u>

What brings you all to Hampton when it's not even Festival Week?

BEA: Well, you want to see the Killer in person, the places where all the killuns were done . . . All the statues and museums.

STELLA: We saw the Shrine to all The Martyrs. They have their photos, and information about their lives up to when they were killed.

MARK: We thought Hampton would be a kind of town, but it's more like a suburb of Melbourne really—Hampton people talk much the same as Melbourne people do.

Are you disappointed?

STELLA: Not me. Hampton's real pretty, I think . . . My husband Ernie had his photograph taken with the Killer.

RAY: Well, I am disappointed. Yes, ma'am. We was under the impression that we would get to see a killun, that it was all very ceremonial, kinda like them bullfights that they have . . . Well, you're Spanish, aren't ya?

No, I'm French.

RAY: Yeah, well we thought that, at very least, we'd get to see the bodies of the dead folks. When the travel agent said that there was a Shrine to The Martyrs, I expected to see embalmed bodies like how the old Egyptians used to do them mummies.

BEA: (LAUGHING) That's just you. You're stupid!

RAY: Who says? . . . These people in Hampton say that they've got a killer, but no one ever gets to see

24

no killuns. He steals out in the dark of night and he kills someone real polite. You never even get to see the blood, just some plaque that the Mayor puts up outside the victim's house. That's not killun! You go t' Fort Worth, you go to Austin . . . Go t' Dallas. Your killers there are real killers. They don't squirrel around in the dark . . . They kill cause they like killun. A real killer enjoys killun because he's a **real** killer. This Killer don't look like no killer I've ever seen. He smiles, he plays with kids. What's the good of having a killer if you're not scared to the crapper of being killed by him?

STELLA: My husband Ernie had his photograph taken with the Killer.

ERNIE: He put an apple on my head and aimed his crossbow at me.

You weren't worried?

ERNIE: Heck no. He's not allowed to kill tourists. **(DISPLAYING APPLE)** Look, he even autographed the apple for me.

RAY: Well, that's just it—If he don't kill tourists . . . If he don't kill journalists from France . . .

We're from Channel 4 in Britain.

RAY: Well, if he don't kill you folks, how can he claim to be a killer? How do we even know that he is a killer if you don't see the bodies?

How do you mean?

RAY: One day a person's there, the next day they're gone . . . The Killer puts his hand up, the police say that he's killed someone. The museum people put another face up in the Shrine . . . Shit, how do we know that the whole thing's not a huge grift?

A hoax?

RAY: Sure it's a hoax! It's tourism! These so-called Martyrs are all sipping cocktails in Barbados, or the South of France. Heck, you probably know some of them.

JOANNE: Ray's just sour cause they don't have no Killin' Festival in Texas.

RAY: Don't talk crap!

MARK: That's the truth, Ray.

RAY: We got **real** killers in Texas! Mean, brutal sonsabitches. You don't get your picture took with no Texas killer. No, ma'am!

8. Tracey Harnett, former girlfriend of Richard Thompson—October 27

<u>Tracey Harnett, a former girlfriend of Hampton's
Killer does not live in Hampton. We filmed her at her
flat in Richmond, an inner suburb of Melbourne. A
heavy smoker, she is a pretty woman with a high
brow, and unusually large green eyes. She had been
reluctant to speak to us because one of her sisters
lives in Hampton, and she feared the consequences of
any criticism she might make of Richard Thompson.</u>

You and Richard Thompson were lovers?

TRACEY: Well, went out together for a year or so
more than a decade back. We were both studying.

What was he like then?

TRACEY: Nice. A bit soft, you know, wimpy. But he
could be charming and intelligent. At his best, he's
quite funny. He was just, I don't know, too sensitive
. . . Thommo was thoughtful in a very self-conscious
way. He was shy, but it wasn't a very endearing sort
of shyness.

**It would have surprised you then to see him become
Hampton's Killer?**

TRACEY: Yes, it did. But Thommo seems to have come
out of himself quite a bit since I knew him. He couldn't
have delivered a speech to a large group of people
then. He was so anxious and panicky.

Why did the two of you fall out?

TRACEY: I knew other boys . . . I wanted to have
fun. Thommo was so serious-minded. We used to argue
a lot.

What about sex?

TRACEY: Was the Killer a deviant, do you mean?

Was he?

TRACEY: He was no Lady Killer. He was nervous . . .
He was pretty keen on me, but he wasn't always the
most functional of lovers . . . It was consistent with

27

his personality then. Thommo was always tense and panicky. But I don't think you could say that he kills people to sublimate his sexual tensions or anything like that.

Did he ever threaten you?

TRACEY: No. Richard's not violent. He's very cerebral. He spends much too much time thinking. I think that he's only ever been attracted to brilliant women. He liked the challenge of brilliant women, but he never really rose to the challenge . . .

You are aware of other girlfriends that he's had since?

TRACEY: Not girlfriends as such. He was always getting infatuated with someone or other. Thommo's a very obsessive person. He used to write hundreds of letters. He was keen on my sister Elizabeth for a time, was mad about a close friend of hers, Francesca Morricone . . . Catherine O'Shaunessy . . . He was crazy about them.

Would he still write to any of them?

TRACEY: He fell out with Liz and Catherine . . . Francesca's dead.

When did she die?

TRACEY: She disappeared while she was travelling in Denmark. There was a big investigation . . . She'd been staying at a Youth Hostel in Copenhagen. She just vanished.

What about Richard?

TRACEY: He was devastated, I think. I heard from friends of his that he hired a private detective to search for her.

Had they been lovers?

TRACEY: God, no! She liked him, and they were close, not close enough for Richard probably . . . He was crazy about her.

Crazy enough to have killed her?

TRACEY: Thommo could be stupid, and intense. But

he couldn't have killed her. I really can't imagine
Thommo hurting anyone.

You can't?

TRACEY: (LONG PAUSE) No, I can't. I know what
you're thinking, but there's a difference.

Between killing neighbours and murdering a friend?

TRACEY: Yes, I think so.

Could you elaborate?

TRACEY: I still feel that I know Richard pretty well.
He's a dag, and he's a schmuck for doing the shit that
he does, but he's not a murderer.

9. Ken Jansz, Statistician—October 27

We filmed Ken in his small office. He's a very dark Sri Lankan man in his mid-forties. Ken sat at his desk, surrounded by computer screens and filing cabinets.

You seem to spend most of your time compiling statistical information concerning the killings . . .

KEN: Yes, the whole thing fascinates me.

How can you justify the time commitment?

KEN: Well, you shouldn't be mistaken, I'm not in this as an amateur. This is a very lucrative business. I supply information to gamblers, bookmakers, interested parties. The Festival is a multi-billion dollar industry, and everything about it requires a totally professional approach.

What kind of statistics do you provide?

KEN: Everything. As you know, there have been thirty-three killings. We provide location breakdowns, time breakdowns, data related to the method of killing, whether or not the persons were known to the Killer socially.

Could you give some specific examples?

KEN: Well, there have been eighteen male victims and fifteen female, never more than four of one sex in succession. All but six of the victims have been killed in their own homes, fourteen during daylight hours, thirteen at night. The crossbow has so far been the Killer's favoured weapon. He's used the crossbow to make seven killings. He hasn't used a gun, or a knife, or cutting weapons. I believe that you get odds of 25–1 on his next victim being killed with a chainsaw. Twelve of the victims had never spoken to the Killer prior to the killing, only eight would have been said to know him reasonably well. The information that I have here breaks down into hundreds of categories and cross-references. Age, religion, race.

How about non-Anglo-Celtic girls aged between twelve and eighteen?

KEN: Two.

Similarity of method?

KEN: None—One smothered, one poisoned.

What's all this information leading to?

KEN: Predictability . . . We don't really hope to uncover an exact method . . . There's the Paradox of Schrodinger's Cat for a start. We know that the Killer's actions won't be unaffected by the fact that he's being scrutinised, and that he knows that he's being scrutinised. What I'd hope to offer the people who invest in my service is an increased probability. I don't believe in absolute randomness. That is, I don't believe the Killer could be operating by a method that's perfectly random. There's got to be an imperfection there somewhere, some kind of fear or favour or blindspot. Eventually, I'll catch him out with some sort of pattern; whether it be anagrams based on the initials of the victims' surnames, or a numerical scheme related to their telephone numbers. It's a game of guessing and double-guessing.

The Killer has to be seen to be totally impartial?

KEN: Yes, that's his mandate.

What if it turns out that he's not totally impartial?

KEN: Well, that wouldn't worry me . . . I'm speaking personally now. I'd be much more worried if the Killer really was able to produce a random method of victim selection, or a random application of dissociated random methods.

Why?

KEN: Because it wouldn't be human. It's not even God-like to be so perfectly disinterested or indifferent. Don't misunderstand me, I believe in the Festival. I believe in the importance of the Killer as an agent of the Hampton community's will, but what are we left with if that agent is inhuman?

31

Statistics that don't indicate anything, random numbers.

KEN: Yes, and that concerns me . . . It would totally destroy the gambling industry centred around the Festival if it was accepted that the killings were entirely unpredictable.

Do outsiders buy your information?

KEN: For gambling?

Gambling . . . anything.

KEN: Certainly. There are a lot of people, outsiders mostly, who question the morality of this enterprise, whether it be the morality of the killings themselves, or the morality of the betting that surrounds the Festival . . . I suspect that must be what your film is about, questioning the morality of the Festival. People hope to uncover the Killer's darkest secrets and prejudices through statistical analysis. They'd like to discover that he's a racist, or a misogynist, or an ageist. They'd like to discover that he plays favourites, or that he's been seduced or corrupted. I think that many outsiders desperately need to believe that their society is morally superior to Hampton's form of association.

Would you help outsiders to gather information which might be used to subvert the Festival?

KEN: The Festival's about making Hampton people more prosperous.

At any cost?

KEN: You know the cost. The cost is a matter of public knowledge. Seven lives a year.

But there is also a greater cost—The justification of cold-blooded murder.

KEN: Only if you choose to see it that way. Hamptonians don't see it that way.

10. Charles and Deborah Kaufmann, parents of Angela—October 29

I interviewed the Kaufmanns in the living room of their substantial Bolton Avenue home, a room lined with books and art works, and photographs of their two children. Charles is older, mid-fifties, while Deborah is in her mid-forties.

When was your daughter Angela killed?

CHARLES: Two years ago. Near the end of the third season . . . She was fifteen.

(LOOKING AT PHOTOGRAPH) This is Angela?

DEBORAH: Yes, that's her with her older sister Sharon . . . She was a very pretty girl.

CHARLES: And bright too. She only ever got As. She wanted to be a research scientist.

DEBORAH: Angela was a very gifted pianist. We have a videotape of her playing, if you'd like . . .

Sure, that would be great . . .

DEBORAH: You couldn't get her to practise, but she had a natural gift.

We pause to watch the video of Angela playing the Moonlight Sonata very competently, with feeling.

She plays beautifully . . .

(LONG PAUSE)

Do you resent her death?

CHARLES: It's a terrible thing when anyone dies. Especially when they're young with so much to give.

DEBORAH: There's a grief, a hollowness, but you can't call it resentment . . .

But she didn't have to die . . .

DEBORAH: Angela was very aware of being part of the community, part of the social contract.

Can a girl of fifteen make that sort of decision?

33

DEBORAH: Children in Hampton are asked to contract every year from when they turn twelve. When they turn eighteen, they're forced to decide. They can contract, or they can leave Hampton. It's not like banishment. If they leave, they can visit whenever they like, and they are subject to the same protection as tourists and outsiders. It's just that they can't study or work here.

Please forgive me for being blunt, but I find it incredible that the parents of a brilliant, beautiful fifteen-year-old girl could accept that the community has the right to sanction her killing.

CHARLES: We are a community. We need each other to survive. The life of the individuals can't be seen as something distinct from the life of the community. Angela willingly volunteered to take on the responsibilities of being part of this community.

DEBORAH: We never saw it as a cold-blooded decision to kill Angela. It's a tragic event . . . an impersonal tragedy. If a tree falls on a child and kills her, you don't cut down every tree in town. You don't ban lightning, or cars, or deep pools of water.

But I don't see how you can call it impersonal? A man has entered your home and smothered your daughter. You know who he is. You see your daughter's killer on the street . . .

CHARLES: Other people have been killed. Some are good people, some are not so good. We know that it could have been us, or Sharon, that it still could be any of us . . . The killings give value to our lives. They make us value our lives. Every day is like a glorious bonus. After the seventh killing of the year, when the Festival begins, there's an extraordinary release of joy. It's a genuine, heartfelt thanksgiving.

The Festival has also made you very prosperous.

DEBORAH: Yes, that's true. We run an art gallery on the beachfront. Business is excellent. We've recently purchased paintings by Kandinsky and Marc, and several erotic drawings by Gustav Klimt.

Have you become prosperous at the expense of your daughter's life?

CHARLES: (CONSIDERED PAUSE) I know that outsiders would say that. It's a very simplistic equation . . . It's not just us who have prospered. Everyone has. Hampton's become a wonderful place. Hampton people are closer than any people anywhere. You should have seen what it was like before the Festival.

DEBORAH: Hampton people care about each other. They appreciate that all Hampton people are making a vital contribution . . . They love each other.

But isn't that notion of love and gentleness and affection at odds with the fact of your daughter's murder and the rumours surrounding it?

CHARLES: We don't want to know about any foul gossip . . . We know the truth.

The rumour that Angela was raped before she was killed.

CHARLES: That's a lie! A pernicious lie.

DEBORAH: We saw her body.

CHARLES: It's totally untrue.

If it became known that there was perversity associated with the killings, it would destroy tourism, it would end the Festival . . .

CHARLES: Our daughter Angela was smothered. She died decently, she was treated with respect.

And people made wealthy by the murders might be prepared to keep quiet about an outrage which would threaten their prosperity . . .

CHARLES: (FURIOUS, GETTING UP TO PUSH THE CREW OUT OF THE HOUSE) Who are you to talk of outrage? How can you speak to us like this? . . . These lies, they're cruel fabrications. The propaganda of outside commercial interests. You people can't stand the idea that Hampton people might be content. You

35

have to contaminate happiness wherever you see it, because you don't have the courage or imagination to find your own happiness. These accusations, they're all lies invented by sick people . . . Pathetic, envious perverts.

DEBORAH: You don't want to understand. We trust the Killer. You couldn't know him to spread those lies about him.

The people who'll watch this film only care about the truth . . .

CHARLES: Do they? You know them, do you? Do you really know your audience enough to say that what they really care about is the truth?

11. Richard Thompson, Killer's Annual Speech, Concert Hall, Hampton Casino—October 29

Since the commencement of the Festival, an outstanding casino–conference centre has been built on the site of the former Hampton Community Hall. A sell-out audience of two thousand, most of them tourists, turned out to see an evening of entertainment by Hampton performers which included the local avant-garde band, Approximate Life, and the Killer's third annual speech. He instituted the speech as a means of explaining his various moral and political positions. Even as a former high school teacher, Thompson is a poor speaker, given to reading nervously from a prepared text. Locals jokingly refer to these speeches as his 'sermons from the mount'.

THOMPSON: Some time ago, a friend who no longer lives in Hampton asked me whether I could distinguish between my role here in Hampton and that of the State Executioner in societies where capital punishment still operates. From the tone of her enquiry, I had no doubt that she was unable to differentiate between the two functions. Those of you who have heard me speak before will know my attitude to this. I do not see the Killer as an operative who enforces the moral or legal judgements of this community. To the contrary, the Killer's agency underpins the contractual arrangements binding the community and its individual constituents.

There are many people who come from outside Hampton who argue that all killing is immoral. To that, I say that this community has decided that seven killings done at random each year—and those seven only—are morally justifiable. Our community is agreed that seven killings are essential to safe-guarding the future well-being of Hampton. To put it more succinctly, No Festival, No Hampton.

The rejoinder is predictable enough. Critics insist that if one human life is deemed to be expendable, then all human life is devalued. They say that the seven killings we have decided upon is an arbitrary nomination—that the number might as easily have been two or two thousand—that we are all expendable, and so forth . . . Ultimately, I consider this to be a debate about diction and contradiction. It's a debate about a community's right to define itself, to decide upon its own laws and moral imperatives.

So often when visitors complain that killing is wrong, they say that capital punishment is morally reprehensible, and that even the most heinous criminals should be locked up for life. Superficially, I'd feel inclined to agree with them. Killing people is dirty work. It's entirely undesirable. I'm also quite happy with the argument that capital punishment won't deter capital offences, and that the elimination of criminals won't contribute to the community's sense of life having intrinsic value. But the alternative is that you lock the murderer or rapist away for what, thirty years, forty years, at thirty thousand dollars a year. You're talking a million dollars.

Now, I'm not saying that it's indefensible for a community to spend one million dollars to sustain an imprisoned murderer. However, I am saying that it may be immoral for a community or State to choose to outlay that money on an imprisoned criminal if it is a **choice** between the murderer and the purchase of a humidicrib, or an intensive care ambulance, or research into breast cancer or cot death. **Every community** has to determine its life or death priorities within the limits of its financial resources.

What I'm getting at here is that Hampton is not a unique society, or even a particularly unusual one.

Every society has paid killers. They are persons whose role it is to define and implement life-or-death priorities. They determine who lives and who dies, albeit at a greater distance than I do in my operation.

Let's suppose that you decide to commit your resources to humidicribs. With the technology that we have available now, you can save the lives of babies born fifteen weeks premature. Lots of these babies are kids that would have died without medical intervention . . . That's terrific. A society might even be prepared to wear the fact that these highly premature kids have a much higher probability of illness in later life than your average punter. But where does your benevolence stop? What if you could save the lives of kids who are less than half-term? Somewhere along the line these prem kids could start ringing up very serious outlays for your health system. Will you feel morally constrained to save the little buggers because every human life is uniquely valuable, because every prematurely born kid might be Mozart? To save them whatever the cost?

The problem is that while you're ploughing money into humidicribs to save the kids that nature would have sacrificed, you've emptied your cash register of funds for kidney research or liver research, or for the cancer research that might save a 39-year-old much-loved, much-needed mother of four . . . We're talking very big equations here.

What I'm saying is that every society, every administration, has a dozen or more of these hired killers, but you won't ever recognise them by the big 'K' stitched onto their blazers. The difference here is that Hampton's Killer doesn't hide away in the darkest recesses of a shadowy institution, anonymous and removed. In Hampton, you can be sure that your age or sex or wealth or race or political influence won't be a determinant in your Killer's calculations.

Additionally, the prosperity of our community enables all Hampton people to have access to the very finest health care. This community donates tens of millions of dollars for various forms of medical research, both inside and outside of Hampton. We have a sense of purpose here. There hasn't been a single suicide in Hampton since the inception of the Festival. We believe that life is valuable, and we consider that Hampton's Festival is a **celebration** of the true value of life and association.

But this is no fairyland. Maybe this community is alone in recognising the real relationship between the cost of living, and the value of life.

As you would expect, the wealth and prosperity of our tribe offend those who are not so wealthy, or those whose wealth is built on a less equitable, less democratic foundation. These people are most offended by the unity of our community. Many outsiders feel constrained to depict Hampton as a dangerous and subversive 'other', a sinister death cult. It suits external interests to portray Hamptonians as greedy hillbillies who enjoy the fruits of a hidden shame.

We don't compel people to be initiated into our tribe, and we don't prevent them from dissociating whenever they choose.

When critics argue that Hampton prospers through making killing an entertainment, they demonstrate their failure to grasp the real achievement of our Festival. Tourists don't come to see the killings or the bodies—the killings take place in private, and the bodies are never displayed. What visitors actually come to see—and all our research supports this—is a working model of a happy coherent society, a society at ease with the forces of life and death. People are tired of association through fear and extortion, and they want to see their innermost dreams enacted. They want to experience harmony . . . True harmony.

Never fall into the error of calling Hampton a suburb or a place. The Hampton that I care about—the Hampton that I'd kill for—exists at the intersection of dream and desire, fear and fantasy.

12. Grace Johannsen, Psychiatrist—October 30

We filmed Grace, a young psychiatrist, in her large, luxuriously appointed office, which overlooks the Shrine of The Martyrs. She started her practice in Hampton three years ago. There are four practising psychiatrists in Hampton. Eight years ago there were none.

What struck you about Hampton when you first moved here?

GRACE: Mainly, it was the distance between the myth and the reality. The outside world has this notion of Hampton as a kind of weird socialist cult. If you listen to the local government, or the local residents, they hardly speak a sentence without using the big-C word: Community. The truth is somewhat removed from that—Hampton is a gambler's paradise. It's a mad bull-run. The Council presents the Festival as a means of protecting and preserving the values that Hampton was losing. The Festival is supposed to establish a new tradition and continuity. After living here, and dealing with many clients, my feeling is that the Festival will ultimately produce the opposite, that Hampton will have a high-turnover population. Sure, you have the old residents who want to stay no matter what, but mostly you have a loose association of hit-and-run capitalists masquerading as community-minded citizens. Hampton has already become a haven for business adventurers who want maximum profit in the shortest possible term. If they weren't baring their arses at Death in Hampton, you'd find these same people taking the most outrageous risks on the stockmarket. The irony of the Festival of Killing is that just about **everyone** here is out to make a killing. The Killer might be one of the few people who actually believes in the sugar-coated myths fed to the public.

What do you make of Richard Thompson?

GRACE: He's a curious character. I'm inclined to believe that he's sincere when he says that he's working for the greater good . . . Yet you'll find he's much more the pragmatist than the glassy-eyed idealist. He's quite Machiavellian, actually. The Killer believes that the prosperity of Hampton justifies the means by which it arrives at that prosperity. The truth is that nobody knows a great deal about him. Except that he's a likeable, apparently straightforward bloke. I doubt that anyone but Thompson could convince the public to invest their faith in the Killer as an institution.

But why would someone choose to become the Killer?

GRACE: A desire for power. A sense of powerlessness. A craving for notoriety . . . It could be any of a hundred things. I've heard the Killer say that he took the job because he wanted to save the Hampton he knew as a boy from disappearing. It makes you wonder whether he lives in the past, or an imaginary version of his childhood, and whether he actually **sees** the suburb he's living in now. Nothing has changed Hampton more than the Festival. The Killer seems unaware of the paradox. The very success of the Festival has ensured the disappearance of the old Hampton. You'd be hard pressed to find a community that has altered as drastically as this one. I'm very curious to know how the Killer deals with that contradiction, whether it's something that he could ever allow himself to be conscious of.

And what about the people who choose to live in Hampton, who volunteer to live in the line of fire?

GRACE: I have the view that many of them are people who are inordinately fearful of death. Hampton has a double-edged attraction for a certain kind of personality. It's easy to use the single-minded pursuit of personal fortune as a deliberate distraction from having to deal with your deepest, morbid anxieties.

People want to see material gain as insulation from death. The **process** of gaining in material terms gives people an excuse to postpone questions of meaning, or spirituality. You find that people here define themselves very much in terms of their material acquisitions, or their accumulated fortunes. I'm sure that many of the highest flyers can't differentiate between the possibility of bankruptcy and the possibility of death. They're both much of a muchness. If you can cheat and scrounge and trade your way out of one, then you can do the same with the other.

You make Hampton sound like a panel by Hieronymous Bosch . . .

GRACE: Mmm. You'll find some very medieval behaviour here. Some people have extraordinary superstitions, obsessive-compulsive behaviours only slightly removed from 'step on a crack, break your mother's back'. People who, for reasons best known to themselves, never walk northwards along Hampton Street on a Friday . . . Extreme, ritualised behaviours. People who **must** smile at the Killer whenever they see him, and people who feel constrained to look away. After a while, these crazinesses begin to become local custom . . . You're right. A lot of the behaviour here is very basic, very Bosch.

So why are you here?

GRACE: There's good business to be done here. Hampton has an unusually wealthy clientele who have an unusual need for psychiatric services. And Hampton also presents a unique opportunity for research. I have two books in development, along with a series of papers which analyse my experiences here.

How much of your work involves counselling the bereaved?

GRACE: Surprisingly little. The bereaved tend to buy into the mythology of the Festival. They need to make an emotional investment in the idea of a community made possible through sacrifice. In their grief, Hampton people tend to resist examination of their real underlying motives.

Which are the same as your own, surely?

GRACE: Yes. I can't deny that. To get on. To advance a career. To make money quickly. I'm not going to apologise for that. I don't see myself as morally superior to the other people who have come here.

But you are, as you say, 'out to make a killing'. Morally, your position's no different to Richard Thompson's?

GRACE: That's an interesting question. On the surface, I'd be inclined to agree. I'd have to consider it more closely . . . Just now, you'll have to excuse me. I've been keeping a client waiting.

13. Natalie Sherrin, Bank Manager—October 30

We located Natalie in the extravagantly spacious foyer of the Hampton Bank.

Was it opportunistic to establish a private bank in Hampton?

NATALIE: We were responding to an immediate demand . . . It was a unique situation. In the early years of the Festival, there were lots of people from outside Hampton who wanted to invest in Hampton businesses, or wanted to set up business in Hampton to capitalise on the Festival . . . But then you began to get a diametric shift. It only took twenty months for there to be so much wealth in the hands of Hampton people that they needed a bank that could respond to their specific investment needs.

There is a phenomenal amount of wealth here . . .

NATALIE: Yes. It's like a small oil state, a Brunei or Kuwait, the only difference being that the wealth is more widely distributed here.

Is it possible to put that wealth into some kind of perspective?

NATALIE: We're forecasting that in ten years time, Hampton people will control ninety per cent of the wealth in the State of Victoria.

That would give a small community an inordinate amount of political influence . . .

NATALIE: Hampton already has that—If international tourism to Hampton stopped, the State's finances would collapse. There's an obvious imperative . . .

An imperative?

NATALIE: Hampton will have to extend its domain to keep pace with its financial growth and political influence.

So you envisage that a suburban Festival of Killing will eventually become a Melbourne Festival of Killing as Hampton's investments come to dominate the city?

46

NATALIE: Dominate the State. Hampton will become the seat of power. It's virtually inevitable that Melbourne will become as geographically subordinate to Hampton as it is politically and economically subordinate. Sooner or later, a major realignment is going to take place. Melburnians will fall under the extended control of the Hampton administration, whether they approve of the Festival or not.

You mean that it will become impossible for Melbourne people to dissociate, even if they regard killing to be morally indefensible?

NATALIE: That's pretty much the case already. The people in Melbourne depend on the killings as much as the people in Hampton do. It's like living in one of those cities on the Danube or the Rhine. You cop the flow-on from what happens upstream, whether you like it or not. You can't contain the consequences of something like the Hampton experiment. If you live in Greater Melbourne, the Hampton Festival is going to change your life whether you approve of the killings or not.

A Domino Principle.

NATALIE: I guess . . . You can't insulate yourself from what's happening next door.

But what would economic expansion or colonisation do to the unity of purpose in a small community like Hampton?

NATALIE: Ultimately, I'm a pragmatist. I'm a banker. My pragmatism inclines me to the view that community interests will always be subordinate to financial interests. There's a lot of myth-making that goes on here. When Hampton people rationalise the killings, they tell you that Hampton's not very different from anywhere else . . . And that's just what I'd say too—Hampton's no different to anywhere else, except that it's got a massive profit generating enterprise. And when that enterprise finally ceases to generate wealth, Hampton people will behave just like people everywhere else.

Early in the afternoon of October 30, the sixth kill of the season took place. Marie Donkersloot, mother of two school-aged children, was killed in her home, shot at close-range by a crossbow bolt that penetrated her heart. Ironically, her husband Piers is a heart surgeon at Hampton's recently opened Community Hospital.

The conventions of the week-long period of mourning prevented us from interviewing Piers. He and his young family emigrated from South Africa four years ago. The renovated and extended weatherboard home in Mills Street that they purchased for $812 000, had been sold at auction for $288 000 just three years earlier.

Though we received permission to film the funeral parade, we were prevented from taking shots inside the church or the cemetery. In order to keep faith with the usual discretions following a killing, Richard Thompson cancelled an interview which had been arranged for November 3. Hampton people also refused to be interviewed in the following week. Though schools close the day after each killing, all businesses continue to operate, reaping the benefit of money brought in by people on pre-arranged package tours, and the thousands of funeral junkies like the Englishwoman, Rachel Manzie.

14. Rachel Manzie, Funeral Junkie — November 4

We filmed Rachel, an Englishwoman in her late-fifties, in the street outside the Shrine of The Martyrs.

You seem to enjoy the funerals?

RACHEL: This is my thirty-fourth. I've been to every funeral.

You actually fly in from Bath for each funeral?

RACHEL: They're extraordinary . . . so moving. An unbelievable level of sacrifice. All thirty-four of these people bound together by their civic-mindedness.

And bound together by a single killer?

RACHEL: Yes, that's right.

Are you a religious person?

RACHEL: Yes, very.

Then how can you reconcile your Christian convictions with this morbid celebration of killing . . . With a man putting himself in the place of God?

RACHEL: Do you think that's what's happening?

What do you think is happening?

RACHEL: Something extraordinary, something magical. It's an appreciation. You'll begin to feel it yourself when the preparations for the Festival begin . . . In the next day or two, they'll start decorating the streets. All the colour, the excitement and anticipation . . . It's like no other place on earth. Your senses become rarefied, appreciative. It's exactly like the world must have been at the very outset. In Paradise. Joys occasionally interrupted by the voice of God. It's a real festival. It's very medieval. Where else would you get a more powerful sense of God's presence in the world?

That's fine, so long as the autographed bolt of lightning doesn't have your name on it . . .

RACHEL: I don't think that you understand. I think that you have a problem with the Festival because

49

you're not a religious person. You don't have a cosmic intuition.

Why don't you come to live in Hampton?

RACHEL: I would. I'm on the waiting list. But by the time the opportunity comes around, I'll be sixty-five or older, and beyond starting a business here. It's business people they want in Hampton, not potential Martyrs.

15. 'Michael', Professional Gambler—November 5

Our meeting with 'Michael' was a breakthrough. Until then, we had only been able to find Hampton people who supported the Festival, or those who had mild reservations about its morality. 'Michael' was able to lead us into the dark side of Hampton. Concerned that his identity be kept secret, we gave 'Michael' assurances that interview footage would not be released before the end of this year. The interview was filmed in a hotel room in Williamstown, a suburb on the other side of the bay from Hampton. Throughout the short session, 'Michael' wore a gorilla mask, and that, combined with poor audio levels, will probably necessitate the addition of subtitles over the footage.

How long have you been involved in gambling in Hampton?

'MICHAEL': I've had a casual interest there since the Festival began, but in the last two or three years I've been pretty much full-time.

Do you make money?

'MICHAEL': I haven't cashed-in yet, but I make money. As a consultant, mostly. I pass on my opinions and judgements. I make very few bets myself . . . You'll find that there are lots of people who'll bet on anything—The date of a killing. The hair colour of a victim. I prefer to observe and wait. The biggest part of a bet is choosing what you bet on. You have to keep things within your sphere of expertise. By the time I decide what it is I'm going to bet on, it's not a gamble any more.

How do you do that?

'MICHAEL': I watch the Killer very carefully.

Do you stalk him?

'MICHAEL': No. Of course, you have people who try that. But they're kidding themselves. You've got to read the Killer's personality. The important thing is not to understand what he is or what he does, but what he **thinks** he is, and how he wants to be seen. He knows that he needs to be seen as impartial, but a question of nerve comes into that. Even impartiality has a time-frame. You ask yourself would he really be prepared to kill three or four sixty-year-olds in a row, even if a random method told him that he had to, because by doing that he'd allow the **suspicion** of partiality or prejudice to undermine people's confidence in the Festival. Perception is more important than reality. He has to be constantly double-guessing. The Killer will have long-term considerations and short-term ones, and there have to be times when these conflict. That's what I'm waiting for, the moment of vulnerability, the loss of nerve, the loss of self-belief. I'm slowly developing an intuition with regard to his misgivings . . . I keep a close eye on what books and magazines he reads, and the films he watches.

I can imagine how you could find out what he's buying, but how can you know what he reads, or what he actually watches?

'MICHAEL': You can find out anything about the Killer. There's always someone who has the information that you want, or someone who can get it for you.

But how is it possible to regulate the gambling in Hampton if confidential information can be purchased?

'MICHAEL': It's not possible! The regulations are a fucking joke! I can't believe that people believe in a suburban council's capacity to regulate a gambling industry of this size. The whole Festival is corrupt. Hampton is dominated by the crime bosses.

The Council?

'MICHAEL': Crime operates at every level. From the 'genuine' citizens who run shelter companies that expatriate profits to criminal organisations outside Hampton, to the councillors in the pay of those organisations who help to facilitate building developments. Then there are the strictly illegal activities: protection rackets, money laundering, drug trafficking, prostitution . . . It's all there. In a big way. The public view of Hampton is that it's a worthy social experiment, that it's separate from the real world. The truth is, Hampton **is** the real world, only more so. Everything that's wrong and evil in the real world exists there in concentration. Wherever you have big money, you're going to attract the interest of disreputable people who want a piece of the action.

How does organised crime corrupt the Festival?
'MICHAEL': Fear. Extortion. In terms of hard dollars, tourism is just a piddle. The most lucrative part of the Festival is gambling, so that's also where Hampton is most vulnerable. As soon as the Festival proved itself as a money-making concern, the Council found itself under threat of terrorist attacks on the main tourist hotels . . . What would you do? You buy peace. And once you've made a secret transaction to preserve the integrity of your Festival, you set in motion an endless series of extortions and pay-offs. Not even the people who make the payments could tell you how much of the income raised by the Festival gets siphoned off to crime bosses in other countries. It's like the island of Grenada experimenting with socialism, and having its tiny economy boycotted out of existence by the Yanks. The Yanks couldn't afford the risk that socialism might be seen to work, not at any level. Only a very naive community could imagine that it would be able to stand apart from the forces which corrupt and contaminate the world. Look at the people on the streets of Hampton. How many of them are locals, how many are tourists, and how many are ghosts?

Ghosts?

'MICHAEL': Operatives, couriers, private detectives, pimps, drivers, bodyguards, pushers, bent detectives . . . The friendly jolly suburb you see on the surface is an illusion. If Hampton ceases to interest the big bosses, if the main game moves elsewhere, then Hampton and its killing spree will dissolve overnight. How do you think that the legislation that allowed Hampton to secede came into being? Not through demand from the Australian public. Certain inducements and advantages were made available to Federal politicians . . .

Why are you speaking to us?

'MICHAEL': I'm a gambler. I'm compulsive.

What are you going to bet on?

'MICHAEL': I'm betting that truth will catch up with the Killer.

Could you be more specific?

'MICHAEL': The truth is specific enough. You might not know the truth when you're looking for it, but you'll always know the truth when you find it. Sooner or later, the Killer's going to see the distance between what he thinks he is, and what he is.

And then what?

'MICHAEL': That's the question. And then what?

16. 'K', Prostitute—November 6

<u>'Michael' put us into contact with 'K', a very articulate Japanese–American prostitute who has an Australian mother. We filmed her in the room of an expensive Hampton hotel where she conducts her business. A woman in her early-twenties, she was very nervous, and smoked throughout the interview. We shot 'K' in silhouette. Despite her Asian appearance, she has a pronounced American accent.</u>

How long have you been working as a prostitute in Hampton?

'K': Three years.

Is prostitution common here?

'K': Officially, there's no prostitution in Hampton. Street prostitution's illegal, and it's heavily policed.

Unofficially?

'K': It's rife. The brothels are very highly organised. There's a trade-off between the crime bosses and the Hampton authorities. If you're known to work for the right boss, the police look the other way.

The police have been corrupted?

'K': (LAUGHS LOUDLY) Everything here is bent! There's big money in Hampton. Rich tourists expect girls. They expect to get anything they're prepared to pay for. Girls that will have sex with them. Girls that will be filmed having sex with them. Girls they can tie up and torture . . . Most of the girls are Asian. You get local girls, or girls from other parts of Australia trying to do business in Hampton, but it's dangerous if you're not tied to a big boss . . . Girls just disappear.

Murdered?

'K': Sure.

By the crime gangs?

'K': By the police, by the gangs, same thing. The vice has to be kept concealed. The amateur prostitutes would draw people's attention to the possibility of corruption.

Have you been forced to work here?

'**K**': Not forced . . . Coerced. I have expensive habits.

You could stop working if you wanted to?

'**K**': I wouldn't need to work here if I didn't shoot smack. But I'm not sure that I could give up smack and give up work and expect to live. Girls are a very good business in Hampton. The people that I work for don't like people messing with their revenue . . . Hampton is supply and demand. There's lots of people with lots of money to spend, and lots of them have exotic tastes. Young girls. Young boys. If you want something badly enough, there's someone here who can get it for you.

Drugs?

'**K**': Are you joking? **(EMPHATIC)** The only reason they cover up the prostitution's to cover up the fact that the prostitutes are a cover for the people who run the drugs . . . Don't listen to what people tell you . . . You have no idea how much money comes through this place. It's Fantasyland. And your head has to be in Fantasyland to think that you can have this much money around and people aren't going to get bent. The Festival's about making money through killing people. It's dirty money, so Hampton people can hardly complain if there's dirty money about.

So, everyone has a price?

'**K**': Well, yeah . . . In my experience.

Could the Killer be bought off?

'**K**': Sure. But why would anyone want to? The crime organisations don't need to buy the Killer. They have everyone they need. Better to let the Killer do his duty thinking that he's being honourable. He kills all these people, but he might be the most decent person in this town. Decent but dumb. Dumb enough to believe that he's a hero.

17. Richard Thompson, Mario's Restaurant—November 7

<u>We interviewed Thompson while he ate a large plate of fettuccine with mushrooms at Mario's, an elegant, old-fashioned Hampton restaurant. Thompson's personal assistant indicated that he had recently received bad news about the death of a friend overseas, but he displayed no sign of being distracted.</u>

Is it good?

THOMPSON: Mmm.

Are you a vegetarian?

THOMPSON: (MOUTH FULL) Not on your life!

We filmed your speech—This idea of tribalism . . . Do you see yourself as the equivalent of a tribal witchdoctor?

THOMPSON: Well, I'm no anthropologist or sociologist . . . I'm more concerned with the kind of moral judgements that are made about the Killer's role, and the community, and the paradoxical situations of the people who make these judgements. I can understand people wanting to intervene if Hampton was in a constant state of civil conflict, or if Hampton people were crying out that they were being persecuted or coerced. But where are the unhappy people? Think about it. A Hampton person related to a Martyr could make a fortune by spilling their guts against the Killer or condemning the Festival . . . Much more money than most could hope to gain commercially. So why don't they do it? We have a fixed set of laws that we as a society have agreed to. Is there a community anywhere in the world that has a greater sense of purpose, of cohesion? The central tenet of our association is that seven citizens are killed each year. No one is forced to associate.

It's just that you raised the tribal thing, and I suppose that if you were looking to compare your tribe with an

Aboriginal tribe, you'd say that Aboriginal societies operated a system that was sustainable over a long period of time, but your system, killing for the entertainment of gamblers and tourists, is much like the circus. Once the routine of the Festival becomes too familiar, or too exposed, the profitability of the operation must fall into decline. Already, you have the Hampton Festival of Killing being emulated in cities in Asia, and the former Eastern Bloc.

THOMPSON: I don't see that the circus example is relevant . . . This is more a matter of ritual and tradition. Ceremony. To say that it's killing for entertainment is too reductive. Being the first Festival of Killing, we have every chance to outlast our imitators. **(PARODYING ADVERTISING SLOGAN)** Ours is the authentic Festival, recognised throughout the world . . .

I asked you earlier whether you thought that it was wrong to kill, and in your lecture you defended your role on pragmatic grounds. What about your ideal philosophical position?

THOMPSON: I don't believe in black and white positions. Every situation is distinct. The rightness or wrongness is dictated by a specific context.

Could that apply to a murder, to a crime of passion where a man murders a lover who has disappointed or betrayed him?

THOMPSON: Your example's too vague. That's where the worst errors are made: categorisation, generalisation. Details are everything.

What happened to your friend Francesca Morricone?

THOMPSON: (MATTER-OF-FACT) Francesca vanished.

Was she murdered?

THOMPSON: I don't know . . . Probably. What I know is that she stopped writing to me.

Maybe she accidentally wandered into a communal

society that permits the murder of seven strangers a year?

THOMPSON: (SOUR) You'll have to work on that. What Freud says is true, a joke's only a joke when the audience laughs . . .

But that would be one of your paradoxical moral situations, wouldn't it, if the Killer, the white knight of society, turned out to be a base murderer?

THOMPSON: I didn't murder Francesca . . . I was crazy about her. We had a falling out. She left for overseas. I expected that she would write, but there were no letters. Something awful happened to her.

Do you feel guilty?

THOMPSON: Yes, I do feel guilty. I might have said something, done something that drove her away . . .

Should I feel guilty? . . . Being alive is a kind of complicity. We're all accomplices and collaborators in every foul deed.

Who are you?

THOMPSON: Who are you to ask? . . . Christine, I think that you should tell me what distinguishes a journalist, a writer, a coroner, or an historian from a socially sanctioned killer. You've begun with the presumption that what I do is wrong. I could just as easily adopt a position which presumed that journalism, or pathology, or historical enquiry were morally abhorrent and unjustifiable. We're living in the quantum age. It's time that you learnt to embrace relativity.

It might also be time for you to acknowledge what's going on around you . . . We've spoken to people who've told us that the Hampton Festival is entirely corrupt: that the Council and police are obedient to the interests of organised crime, that Hampton traders are under the thumb of gangsters demanding protection money.

THOMPSON: Protection from me?

Protection from Mafia retribution.

THOMPSON: Mafia! Look, I don't know who you've

been talking to, but, all this stuff. It's puerile fabrication . . . There's been rumours of Mafia operations since Day One, but if organised crime was here, I'd know about it. If the Festival was known to be corrupt, the Killer would be reviled, not celebrated. People would be leaving in droves. It's all part of the game of subversion. Outside business interests. Outside pressure groups. They refuse to leave us alone. There are a tremendous number of people who want to undermine the Hampton Festival . . . You're going to end up being very confused if you believe everything that people tell you in Hampton.

Why wouldn't organised crime be attracted to Hampton?

THOMPSON: You want to believe that the Festival could be corrupted or debased. That's been your slant from the beginning . . . Sure, there are circumstances under which a Festival like this could be corrupted. But what would that mean? **Think about it** . . . It might mean that Hampton people were too naive, that the Festival was ill-conceived, or not worth the risk. But I think that it would also mean that a good and harmonious society is impossible to achieve, because corruption and contamination are inevitable. You'd be saying that evil and chaos are irresistible and dominant forces in the universe. Of course, if you accept that, it follows that you advocate a fatalistic policy of surrender, that people shouldn't even **try** to construct a better version of society, because all your best intentions are destined to be foiled. Is that what you want?

I'm interested in the things that are actually happening here . . .

As I began to make my point, there was a sequence of loud explosions in the street outside the restaurant . . .

60

Jesus, what was that? A bomb?

The other restaurant patrons began to applaud wildly, and burst into song.

THOMPSON: No, I don't think so . . . **(VERY AGI-TATED)** They're fireworks.

Thompson moved away from the table, motioning for the maitre d', then requesting that a telephone be brought to him.

What's going on?
THOMPSON: I don't know . . . I'm sorry. I'll have to cut short the interview.
Is something wrong?
THOMPSON: The fireworks signal the seventh killing. It's the beginning of the Festival . . .
Has there been a seventh killing?
THOMPSON: Look, I'm sorry . . .

We tried to follow Thompson as he was escorted away through the kitchen by the maitre d', but the door was closed on our camera.
Though it was past eleven on a cold, wet night, crowds were flooding onto the streets, popping champagne corks, twirling brightly coloured umbrellas. Rock and jazz bands were driven through the streets on the back of floats. People danced, and embraced, and drank. The night sky was filled with exploding fireworks and duelling laserlights.
We tried to follow Richard Thompson's car, but we lost him in the throng of people. Quite by accident, we came across a fleet of police and emergency vehicles in Chiselhurst Road, just as a body was being loaded into the back of an ambulance. We tried to approach the premises, only to be barred by police. From where

I stood, I could see a pool of blood in the driveway of number fifteen. After several deflections, we were able to waylay Chief Inspector Ptsouris.

18. Inspector Nick Ptsouris, Scene of Killing, Chiselhurst Road — November 7

What's going on?
NICK: It appears that there has been a murder. A young woman has been bludgeoned with an axe.
It's not the seventh killing?
NICK: No. We don't believe so.
What about the fireworks?
NICK: There's been a stuff-up. Our people were notified that the seventh killing had taken place.
Notified by the Killer?
NICK: Apparently not.
But there's a special phone. A code.
NICK: We'll have to look into that . . .
So someone's deliberately faked the seventh killing?
NICK: It appears that way.
As a practical joke? Sabotage? What?
NICK: Look, it could be any of a hundred things . . . You'll have to excuse me. This is pretty deep shit.
You've spoken to Richard Thompson?
NICK: Only very briefly.
What did he say?
NICK: That he had nothing to do with any killing . . . It's much too early for a start . . . It's not even summer.

It has since come to light that the victim was the young prostitute, Keiko Morimoto, daughter of the famous American performer Kohji Morimoto, and previously interviewed as 'K'. She was murdered by a single killer as yet unknown. The police believe that the murderer comes from outside Hampton. How the murderer obtained the killer's codes has not yet been determined. There was no evidence of a break in at Richard Thompson's home. Theoretically, the Killer's codes are known only to Thompson and senior police officials, though it is not inconceivable that they could have been obtained by the security staff who guard Thompson's home.

Since no person or group has claimed responsibility for the murder as a deliberate attempt to sabotage the Festival, most speculation centres on the likelihood that the crime is connected to a betting plunge. It is widely rumoured that unusually large bets were placed on the day prior to the murder, and that many millions of dollars changed hands before the festivities were curtailed.

Another possibility is that the murder was the work of a psychotic copycat. The Hampton Police have since disclosed that an unpublicised murder took place in Orlando Street in March. At the time, they attributed the motive to burglary. Hampton residents have already set up a lobby group whose concern is to determine whether other crimes may have been covered up as a concession to tourism and business.

For their own part, Hampton Council and the Tourist Authority are struggling to keep a lid on the ill-feeling engendered in Japan. Japanese cancellations are said to be running at sixty per cent. At the same time, Hampton officials need to deal with feelings of bad faith among foreign tour operators. The Hampton Tourism Authority sells December as the most likely date for the Festival. Even the possibility of leakage into November would be enough to make foreign operators go cold on selling Hampton's Festival as a major international event. Whatever the actual outcome, this debacle has undermined confidence in the ability of the current administration to organise a multi-billion dollar event.

By far the most damaging rumour is that Richard Thompson intends to resign as Killer prior before the seventh killing takes place. Thompson is said to be dismayed that internal gambling interests were behind the murder, or that a sequence of copycat murders might jeopardise the social contract.

I still don't think that one can rule out the possibility that Thompson was behind the murder, using an agent to divert our attention from the allegations of perversity made against him.

Thompson failed to appear at an interview we had arranged for this morning. His personal secretary indicated that Thompson had been required to attend an urgent meeting with the Mayor. We have rescheduled a meeting for Tuesday.

I am trying to line up interviews with the Morimoto family. Kohji and Suzanne Morimoto will arrive tomorrow to take Keiko's body back to San Francisco.

Naturally, Michael, I will keep you informed of any further developments.

Christine Marker
Hampton
November 10–11

The day after Christine Marker's transcripts were sent to London by international courier, three members of her Channel 4 film-crew, Michael Tynan, Penny Donaldson and Gillian Chatterton, were found murdered in their hotel rooms. Each had been bound with cord before having their throat cut. Christine Marker had vanished. Bloodstains in Marker's room were consistent with her having been executed in a manner similar to her colleagues.

The initial coronial inquest, presided over by the Hampton Coroner, Helen O'Brien, determined that the crimes were highly likely to have involved Hampton's Killer, Richard Thompson. Forensic evidence presented to the coroner argued that bloody footprints found at the crime scene were produced by a pair of white Diadora sports shoes found in Richard Thompson's bedroom.

The subsequent Elliot Commission, while not absolving Thompson, found that there had been serious irregularities in the conduct of the coronial inquiry. Elliot criticised the failure to have the forensic evidence examined by an independent agency. He considered that too much weight had been given to testimony that the letter written by the person purporting to be Morimoto's killer* was the product of Richard Thompson's desktop printer. That of itself was far from sufficient to establish Thompson's involvement in the conspiracy to kill Morimoto. In Elliot's view, the murder of the documentary crew was likely the work of as many as six assailants. Elliot dismissed as not credible the evidence of three eyewitnesses who had previously testified to having seen Richard Thompson in the vicinity of the crime scene late on the evening of November 11.

---

* The '33 With a Bullet' letter is reproduced in the Appendices.

The more recent Witherspoon Commission found that the murders and disappearances were the result of a criminal conspiracy involving officers of the Hampton Council, the Hampton Internal Security Unit, the Central Intelligence Agency of the United States, and Australian operatives in the employ of international crime organisations. The Witherspoon Commission ordered that Lorraine di Stasio, the former Mayor of Hampton; Wendy Billingsley, the former C.E.O. of the Hampton Tourist Authority; Inspector Nick Ptsouris, Chief of the Hampton Internal Security Unit, and Raymond Gillespie, Hampton Gaming ombudsman be indicted on charges of having conspired to murder Keiko Morimoto, Penny Donaldson, Michael Tynan, Gillian Chatterton and Christine Marker. The Commission also determined that there was sufficient evidence for di Stasio, Billingsley, Gillespie, and Ptsouris to be indicted on charges of having conspired to murder Richard Thompson. In stating his final recommendations, Justice Witherspoon expressed the view that, on the basis of the evidence put before his Commission, it was impossible to establish the extent of Richard Thompson's knowledge of, or involvement in, criminal activity in Hampton.

PART 2

THE PRINCE

RICHARD THOMPSON'S JOURNAL

To those seeing and hearing him, [the prince] should appear a man of compassion, a man of good faith, a man of integrity, a kind and religious man . . . Everyone sees what you appear to be, few experience what you really are . . .

. . . it cannot be called prowess to kill fellow citizens, to betray friends, to be treacherous, pitiless, irreligious. These ways can win a prince power but not glory.

The Prince, *Niccolo Machiavelli, 1513*

The October segment of Richard Thompson's journal comes close to defining the word controversial. Not since the banning of Phillip Roth's novel *Portnoy's Complaint* have so many Australians held an opinion about a work that so few have had the chance to read.

Initially, heated debate surrounded the authenticity of the document. Hampton's Coroner, Helen O'Brien found it suspicious that Thompson should have commenced a separate volume for the crucial October–November period when the most recent volume of his journal still had ample space to see out the year. All previous volumes of Thompson's journal had spanned entire calendar years.* Was the document genuine? And if so, what was its author playing at?

The debate at the subsequent Elliot and Witherspoon Commissions shifted from questions of authorship to questions of authorial intent. How reliable was Thompson as a narrator of his day-to-day experiences? Were his entries sincere or cynical? The pro-Thompsonites hold that the journal proves Thompson's innocence, while their opponents argue that Thompson has skilfully designed a journal that would provide an alibi for his criminal complicity.

We do know that Richard Thompson was bound by his contract with Hampton Council not to speak, act, or write in a manner that might compromise the Killer's methodologies. As a consequence, many legal and professional minds have scoured this disarmingly modest and detached

---

* Readers wishing to examine the previous volumes of Thompson's journal are advised to read Miranda Murray's *If Looks Could Kill: The Diaries of Richard Thompson*.

memoir in the hope of uncovering a key to Thompson's actual opinions. Most intimates of Richard Thompson insist that this cigar is nothing more than a cigar. Others argue a belief that Thompson actually kept a second, frank journal (possibly on disc) which recorded the Killer's activities and private thoughts in fine detail. No physical evidence has emerged to support the existence of a second journal. However, both Commissions were keen to emphasise the fact that Thompson wrote all his correspondence on personal computer, and that the discs which contained that correspondence have disappeared, presumably removed at the same time that Thompson vanished.

Did Thompson use his handwritten journal to construct an elaborate front? The extreme naivety he displays in the journal often seems at odds with his intelligent self-consciousness. Thompson toys with ambiguity and ambivalence. He frequently meditates on the possibility of constructing an alternative version of himself through a fictional journal. The Elliot and Witherspoon Commissions spent a total of eight months debating just how artful, careless, innocent, or cynical Thompson may have been in his choice of words or subject matter. His every phrase was examined for a subtext, alternative meaning, or pointed shift of tone. Thompson's journal seemed to beg the interpretation of forensic experts, psychiatrists, and literary scholars, and the Commissioners duly sought those interpretations.

Richard Thompson's inelegant prose has become the most scrutinised in modern Australian literature. Yet none of the experts has been able to unravel the mystery of Thompson's narrative situation or intent, nor have they been able to interpret his journal in such a way as would establish his guilt or innocence beyond reasonable doubt.

Concentration on legal and ethical matters has tended to overshadow reappraisal of the Killer's character. The most commonly accepted view is that Richard Thompson was well meaning but ingenuous.

I share the view expressed by Laura Davison in her book *Cannibalism for Beginners*. Though Thompson found persuasive rationalisations for his actions, he was preoccupied with the impression he made, and his charm acted to mask dishonest and self-aggrandising tendencies.

According to Davison, Thompson confuses virtuosity— his capacity to perform his duties skilfully—with virtue, or moral excellence. In the journals we see Thompson attempt to persuade himself that he is an author, and that his 'authorisation' entitles him to dispose of minor characters at will. If the killings were intended to unite the Hampton community, they also provided a means by which Thompson could set himself apart from his fellow citizens. I am inclined to regard this distancing process as a measure of Thompson's unconscious contempt for the people who chose to trust and revere him.

The journalist Michael Phillips claims he once asked Thompson whether the Killer ought to be excluded from the random method by which Martyrs are chosen, to which Thompson responded, 'What purpose is served by treating the shepherd as one of the sheep?'*

Whether or not Phillips quotes Thompson accurately, the statement is consistent with the Thompson that we encounter in the journal. The final instalment of his

---

* Michael Phillips, 'The Dark Shepherd' in Russell/Campbell (eds) *Approximate Life: The Enigma of Richard Thompson*. Miranda Murray disputes the attribution of this statement to Thompson, arguing that it is uncharacteristically arrogant. Murray believes that the statement was made by Wendy Billingsley, and that Billingsley was mistakenly presumed to have been quoting Thompson. See intro. to *If Looks Could Kill*.

journal reveals a character whose interests and ambitions are more aristocratic than democratic. Thompson constructs himself as a non-elected head of state: The Prince who bestows favour or disfavour. His fatal inability to predict, recognise, or confront the criminal operations enveloping his office are in large part a consequence of his desire to place himself above the political fray. Hence Thompson's disinclination to challenge expected (but unenforceable) discretions in his private journal. Thompson is not merely protecting the Killer's secret methodology, he is protecting palace secrets. He celebrates his superior otherness.

Clearly, any reading of Thompson's journal must be coloured by knowledge of subsequent events, and I ought to emphasise that my views are at odds with many respected scholars who see Thompson as not merely a folk hero, but as a modern literary hero, an author who demonstrates phenomenal wit and honesty.

At least a wider public now has the opportunity to examine the final segment of Thompson's journal and to construct its own version of the author (or authors).

The reader may now ask, Who is this Killer? Are these the meditations of a foolish egotist, a madman, or an heroic visionary? How genuine is this man who appears so obsessed with the possibility of heroic action, and the myths surrounding his own heroic status? Or are these journal entries merely the cold calculations of a murderer who seeks to veil his crimes by pretending to be a latter-day Camus? If so, we must ask whether this is a Camus expressing his (implied) views of Meursault, or a Meursault impersonating his murdered author?

From Richard Thompson's Journal

OCTOBER

I want to be away from here, to be in Paris at New Year, eating crepes from corner stalls, able to look at people's faces without having to imagine whether I will hear their last words. To eat pastries and drink wine and move freely without scrutiny. To find a place where I can be outside of myself . . . Can it be true that the Russian Csar, Peter the Great, once threw a New Year's Eve party that only ended when all the food and grog ran out in April?

* * *

According to a Sydney radio commentator, the killings are a hoax. This hoax theory has it that the so-called Martyrs have been 'disappeared' to some comfortable foreign outpost to be sustained by secret bank accounts. I don't understand why people are so determined to fly in the face of reason, why they need to construct these metaphoric heavens and afterlives.

* * *

Some training as a clown would have been invaluable. I was doing a photo call at Disney's, and the photographer, from a German magazine, was dissatisfied with the conventional poses. 'Can I ask you now to—how do you say?—*juggle* the weapons?' I picture this man at Yalta with Stalin, Churchill, and Rooseveldt—'Would you mind making for me a human pyramid?' Churchill asks an aid to hold his cigar as he gets down on all fours . . . Then there are the people, and I'm not just talking about tourists, who expect that I should be able to speak every known language. They approach me speaking Greek or Urdu, convinced that I will understand them. They assume that the Killer must be extraordinarily qualified. Languages and formal academic qualifications were never mentioned at the interview. The panel already knew that I'd been an English teacher. I do recall Tom Mitchell[1] asking, 'Have you ever had any psychiatric illnesses?'

'Would it help if I had?' I was surprised that my smartarsery stopped them from pursuing the question. Maybe it didn't matter to the Council that their Killer was a psychopath, so long as he signed autographs, posed for photos, and didn't look like a psychopath, all wild-eyed and foaming at the mouth—Jack Nicholson in overdrive.

* * *

Justine S.[2] has written again saying that she is prepared to offer two million for a 60 000 word memoir. She will send a writer to ghost it if I prefer. She has yet to make clear what kind of autobiography she has in mind. Perhaps she wants a quickie after the fashion of the books written by sporting champions: the usual fake modesty and measured self-denigration—'Did I

---

1 Tom Mitchell, Acting Education Officer, Hampton City Council. Mitchell's older brother, Con, was killed in particularly dramatic circumstances in the second year of the Festival.

2 Justine Scott of Baird Publishing. In testimony before the Elliot Commission, Scott denied having made a two million dollar offer to Thompson for his memoirs. Scott was subsequently convicted of perjury when the letter detailing a two million dollar offer surfaced. She was gaoled for six weeks.

tell you how me and the boys went out an' got totally ratshit after I'd strangled my old primary school teacher?'—I could betray a few locker-room confidences—'Say, did I tell you the one about the famous European leader who offered me an honorary doctorate from an esteemed institution if I would supply him with a videotape of one of the killings?' . . . 'So long as the victim is a young girl, you understand.'—I could write a memoir full of all that Boys' Own stuff (*The Bumper Boys Book of Killing*?), about how the job nearly got on top of me, how I often thought about throwing in the towel, but somehow managed to hang on in there to make the best killings of my career. Of course, it never does to boast in a sporting autobiography, or to set yourself up as some kind of high achiever. Everything has to be reduced to the natural, to be depicted as something that any ordinary bloke could have done if he'd been put in the same position. Sporting autobiographies are a guilty pleasure of mine. I read them the same way that academic friends like to read crime fiction, or romantic novels. You'll find more between the lines in a sporting autobiography about what Australians imagine it is to be Australian, or to be heroic, than you'll find in most serious historical or sociological explorations of the national psyche. The truth is that there is nothing particularly heroic in what I do. Why should I write about it? To what extent should an intelligent person be complicit in the creation of their own myth, or in an uncritical addition to the national myth?

* * *

I once wanted to believe that I was invincible, that I could alter anything by imposing the force of my will, that I could rearrange the world so that I would be relocated at its centre, at its heart. This need for invulnerability had less to do with a power to effect change than it had with the desire to feel that I was absolutely necessary. I wanted to believe that I had been willed into being for a specific purpose. Then I realised that the essential thing was the part that had been written for me, that the part was everything, and that within the part Richard Thompson was annihilated. I am subservient to the role that I play. Beyond that role, I am nothing.[3]

* * *

There is a piece of graffiti scrawled on the bakery in Thomas Street:

HOW WOULD YOU RECOGNISE TRUE EVIL?

I remember a radio talkback host once asked me to define true evil, and the only thing that came to mind was beetroot. Beetroot is evil. Not the flavour so much as the combination of that colour and that texture. If you want to make the world a happier place, if you want to relieve global tension, you could start by eradicating beetroot.

* * *

I'm getting fat. I've put on two kilos in the past couple of months, and seven kilos since I took the job. Too many functions, too much wine. I wonder would

---

3 Could Thompson, with his acute understanding of irony, really believe this? So much of the Killer's journal suggests a determination to manufacture a heroic myth that transcends subservience to an understood role or function.

Hampton tolerate a Killer who didn't match the desired image: an active, youthful man who could be projected positively to the tourist market? This is the era of the Health Papacy. A fat and slovenly Killer would look too immoral. A flabby Killer would look like someone who might get pleasure from the act of killing. If you are slim and you've got a good smile, you can sell anything to a society educated to buy things sold by slim people with a good smile. All the initial market research indicated that people wouldn't accept a female killer. It violated their assumption that an admirable woman—whatever her achievements in other fields—was one who was still primarily concerned with caring and nurturing. For fairly obvious reasons, it wouldn't have done to give the role of Killer to a black, or someone from an ethnic or religious minority. What is it about the WASP male that makes people feel comfortable with him as a Killer?

* * *

When I mentioned to Jane S. that she'd promised to have dinner with me, she became nervous and fumbled for excuses: the age difference, how she ought to be studying. None of that seemed to matter when we kissed outside the Gallery after we'd seen the Kandinsky exhibition. I should have taken her home and ravished her then, when my nostrils were full of the scent of her, but spontaneity's never been my strong suit. Everything about my life is premeditated: plots and rehearsals. Jane told me she wasn't sure that she could cope with the attention. And I couldn't pretend that there wouldn't be any attention. As if the press could ignore the Killer's relationship with a sixteen-year-old girl.[4] One of the things that attracts me to Jane is how unimpressed she seems to be by my notoriety . . . Still, I guess that I've been expecting too much, hoping for a (what do you call it?) 'normal sex life'. This is no 9–5 job, but a weird priesthood. Even if celibacy is not asked or expected of me, how is it possible not to be celibate? Killing someone that you were involved with, or had been involved with, would be too much like killing.

* * *

Millicent Mathews from Kaleidoscope Books called. They are compiling an anthology of stories written by non-literary (illiterate?) celebrities, and she is keen that I contribute. I mentioned that demands on my time would make it impossible to write anything new, but that she might be interested in a story I wrote while I was at university, *Schrodinger Puts Out the Cat*. I shouldn't have said anything without checking to see whether I still had a copy of the story. Worse, I now recall what the story was about, and worry that it might be too revealing when published in a context where it would be sure to be read as a sequence of clues and signifiers to the true nature of the Killer— The first-person narrator of the story is an inveterate

---

4 Jane Stevenson was one of Thompson's few romantic interests during his term as Hampton's Killer. In fact, she was already nineteen years old, and denied having told Thompson that she was younger. The psychiatrist Dr Pamela Woodland testified that it would not be inconsistent for a man of Thompson's apparent sexual immaturity to flatter himself by suggesting the power to overwhelm an under-age girl. Woodland argues that Thompson's resistance to sexual entreaties had less to do with moral strength and integrity than it had with his desire to be seen as a latter-day Ghandi.

peeping Tom, expert at concealing himself on verandas and balconies. Though he has become disenchanted with the banality of suburban sex, he is unable to rid himself of his voyeuristic habits. Only when he is at home after the event does he masturbate, during an idealised mental reconstruction of the sex he has witnessed. One night, he happens upon an extraordinary couple whose sexual encounter occurs in the form of a bizarre ceremonial display: circumnavigations, taunts and teases, accompanied by the recitation of erotic poetry, culminating in a fuck of breathtaking intensity. Excited and beguiled by the strange beauty of their lovemaking, the narrator returns to the same balcony night after night, to be further astounded by their theatrical innovations and orgasmic perfection. One day, however, he becomes plagued by the thought that he is no longer an independent witness, that he has become an ingredient in their performance. He believes it possible that they are not only aware of his presence, but that their lovemaking may be for his benefit, that the success of their performance *depends* on his observation and approval. To declare himself would be to risk snapping the thread, but he has to know whether these extravaganzas exist independent of his gaze. Finally, he decides to pay a young man to peer into the lovers' bedroom and report back to him. As the narrator sits in a bar, waiting for this report, he becomes overwhelmed with remorse. What if some kind of perversity or inauthenticity should reveal itself to his third party? What if their divine lovemaking did not touch or impress his agent? Or worse, what would happen if his agent did something to contaminate or terminate this display of sexual pageantry? My story concludes with the increasingly drunk narrator trying to decide whether to kill his messenger before or after he reports what he has seen . . . Tell me, what would the psychiatric world say when they read of this early fascination with dispassionate killing, with this rehearsed association between killing and alienated sexuality?[5] I think that it might be best if I searched out an essay that I wrote in high school, one of those innocent, ineffectual TV parodies that everyone wrote.

*　*　*

The reader will know my efforts to spare these pages from vulgarity, but a word or two must be said about the new toilets at the Gallery of Modern Art. These toilets could flush away an elephant. The power and volume of the torrent is astonishing. You half expect to see honeymooners in anoraks having their photograph taken next to the flush. (Have the Gallery management made an editorial judgement about the patrons of modern art, their capacity to digest anything?) Still recovering from the violence of this flush, you are unprepared for hand-dryers that char-braise your palms with the ferocity of a dragon snort. Squealing pain. In the cafeteria, you see men with their palms wrapped around long glasses of iced water, and you know that these are brethren who made the mistake of not using the towels. In this age of superheroes,

---

5 Millicent Mathews testified that Thompson did not reply to her request, and no physical evidence of the *Schrodinger* story has ever been discovered. While arguing the case that Thompson was involved in Hampton's criminal conspiracy, Mark Lipstein suggested that this story is the first evidence of Thompson using a plant. According to Lipstein, Thompson wrote this volume of the journal specifically to invent a hyper-ironic version of himself as a means of concealing his criminal intent.

this new convenience is not so much a toilet for men, as a toilet for the Man's Man.

* * *

Exactly what is it with these deadshits at the Tourist Authority? They're like zombies, restlessly counterproductive. Now their very zombiness has given rise to a new promotional idea, HAMPTON: CITY OF DEATH. I had a letter from Wendy Billingsley. Would I support the concept of setting up catacombs beneath the Sillitoe Reserve? A series of long underground tunnels where visitors could view the skeletal remains of the Martyrs. Wendy and her morons wouldn't have proposed anything so outrageous if they'd actually visited the Catacombs in Paris. There you see the neatly stacked bones of thousands of ancient Parisiens. Long, tall rows of anonymous skulls and thighbones. You couldn't look at all that undifferentiated mortality, the nobles stacked with the peasants, and imagine that anything in life amounted to a hill of beans (or even a hill of bones). And you wonder how those eighteenth-century Parisiens might have responded to ad agency fuckwits telling them that catacombs were the way to go, that a City of Death had enormous tourist potential. 'It may sound sick and morbid to you now, King Louis, but think long term. You've got to visualise the big picture.'

* * *

Saw H.P. with his wife J.,[6] and their two young daughters in Ludstone Street. They seem like the perfect

6 Initials have been changed for legal reasons.

young family now. He is on the board at the brewery, having made his reputation (and fortune!) marketing The Killer's Beer. J. seemed embarrassed by H.P.'s reluctance to engage me in conversation. What she doesn't know is that, in the second year of the Festival, her husband offered me a six-figure sum to make J. one of the Killer's victims. H.P. stood there looking down, scuffing his foot on the footpath, trying not to make eye contact. 'They sure are terrific kids,' I say. 'You should come around for dinner some night,' J. offered, 'H. is always talking about you.' And I might take her up on that offer too, just to make the prick squirm . . . What pure joy work would be if I could devote myself to terminating the deserving.

* * *

Sarah[7] tells me that numerologically I am a seven, and that sevens are on an emotional and physical low at the moment. Though I don't subscribe to any of that crap, I *am* on a low. Tracey[8] once described me as an ecstatic pessimist, a self-fulfilling prophet of doom. Maybe my autobiography should detail an intended future. A 200-page list of predictions, desires, and fears: the antithesis of the celebrity listing his or her accomplishments—The first *prescriptive* autobiography. 'When I least expect to find romance, a door will open to reveal a slim auburn-haired girl whose silky voice . . .' I like the idea already. Sometimes I seem to have power over my own destiny the way that I have

---

7 Sarah. Unknown. Possibly Sarah Nixon, the wife of one of Thompson's security guards.
8 Presumably Tracey Harnett, Thompson's lover more than a decade earlier. Harnett had been one of Christine Marker's interview subjects. (See interview 8.)

the power to curtail people's lives. So what prevents me from believing in my freedom to be happy?

* * *

There is an old song that I can't stop humming, an early single by E.L.O. One of the lines is 'I can't get it out of my head', but that's not the name of the song,[9] and I'm sure that most of the words I sing have no relation to the original. I need to be careful. On the day I killed A.K., my head was fixed on The Smiths' song 'Big Mouth Strikes Again', and now I can't hear the song without seeing her long red hair emerging from beneath the pillow, and her legs kicking till the life had been drained from them. Music becomes inextricably associated with strong emotions. *A Clockwork Orange* was like that. Hampton people are amused that their Killer is so fond of alternative music, but what would happen if every song I ever loved became associated with a killing?

* * *

Wendy B.[10] sent over a videotape of a new Japanese cartoon series, *K for Killer*, apparently based on my activities. Naturally, this animated Killer has Asiatic features, is physically exceptional, is exceptionally polite to children, and has (for English-speaking audiences) a dubbed American accent. 'Remember kids, we're all in this together!' The cartoon Killer seems to possess a telepathic skill which enables him to

---

9 Thompson is in error. The Electric Light Orchestra song to which Thompson refers is *El Dorado*.
10 Wendy Billingsley, Hampton Tourist Commissioner, later charged with conspiring to murder Richard Thompson.

determine who *deserves* to die. He waits for a crowd to assemble around his newest corpse so that he can deliver a homily. He is a ridiculously authoritative, moral superhero, a man who knows no fear. It's difficult to imagine him being troubled by doubts or dreams.

* * *

I often wish that I wasn't so even tempered. It's not that I don't feel anger, I just don't have a way of expressing anger that makes my infuriation sound reasonable. I'm certainly not spontaneous. Some passion would be good. What could be healthier than to express anger when anger is appropriate? The problem is, people have learnt to read my personality. They know how to get right up my nose. Like Andrew Dawson and his smartarse letters. Andrew was in the year ahead of me at Hampton High, and he was a smug, spoilt little prick then—a forerunner of the smug Yuppies that virtually strangled Hampton, the genuine middle class who thrived enough to betray the values of the middle class. Andrew went on to study law, and lives in Sydney, doing very remunerative work for the Australian-based multinationals who fuck-up the South Pacific. Neither the nature of his work, nor the fact of his Double Bay mansion, has hindered Andrew's run at power within the Labor Party executive, and I'd guess that I've received five or six letters from Andrew every year since the inception of the Festival. Party letterhead, of course. To begin with, he used to describe me as a grubby parasite, a sexual deviant, and an officer of the economic S.S. But when I refused to bite, he shifted to a more subtle, 'constructive' tack. Why can't I see that my community-conscious rhetoric, and superficial idealism, amount to an effective abandonment of *genuine* idealism, that I have not only given (tacit) support to the economic rationalism that has smothered traditional Australian values, I have become the apotheosis of economic rationalist fantasy?—As if a fucking hypocrite like Andrew has ever done a thing to oppose the sovereignty of economic rationalism within his Party, or in his own life. Did Andrew stand in front of the bulldozers as the guts were ripped out of egalitarianism, the bulldozers that ploughed through everything that once symbolised the (lost) Australian middle class, like the old Southern Stand at the Melbourne Cricket Ground, like our old high school, more to the point? If Hampton now stands at the top end of the money society, if the one sacred belief of modern Australian society is that there is no such thing as bad money, then the acceptability of that view was made possible by the treachery of the *nominal* socialists, the wolves in their imported suits. It really pisses me off. I'd earn not one-tenth of what Andrew Dawson does, but I am the class traitor. For caring about people? For caring about the Hampton community, and the need to act decently according to the wishes of that community? I remember things that fuckwit Andrew with his 'acceptable eight or nine per cent unemployment' would never remember. I remember Hampton before its gentrification, when Hampton was the absolute exemplar of middle-class suburban life in Australia. This was before the people who prospered from that life turned on it, their terrible insecurity manifest in the status symbols they bought: the expensive foreign cars, the tasteless mansions that they built. They decided that the state schools that had been good enough for them weren't good enough for their own children, weren't *exclusive* enough, that a state school education wouldn't tell the world that they had enough money to buy the best that money could buy. I cried when the bulldozers demolished Hampton High. I finally had some notion then of what sacred sites might mean to Aboriginal people, that it's a sin to desecrate a site of knowledge and initiation. Those sites have an energy that will never dissipate. Even before there had been any talk of festivals, I knew that I wanted to try to retrieve for this community the idea of Community, to remind them of the *need* for Community before the value and meaning of the concept was entirely washed away by money-cynicism, and status obsession, and exclusivity. It's all very well for a fat slug poseur like Andrew Dawson to say that my success has been to rationalise a community of true economic rationalism, a suburb of economic tyrants. He doesn't live among people. He doesn't know what it is to be touched by people, and to be needed by people. His grand sentiments are just the mask worn by The Apparatus. If he knew people, Hampton people, he would never dare say that the person who finally assassinates Richard Thompson 'will come from Hampton, and that the assassin of the Killer will be a champion of the people, a true hero of our times'.

* * *

Every day the task is to recover the meaning of things, to restore the meaning of things, to preserve the meaning of things, to define and redefine, to make sense of things, or to give sense to things, to battle against the habit of just being, just doing. It's the battle against chaotic meaninglessness, against being overpowered by ripples set in motion by a butterfly fart in Kalimantan . . .

* * *

An extremist lobby group in New York has started a rumour that a disproportionate number of Hampton's victims have been gay, lesbian, or bisexual, and that the Hampton Festival of Killing is a front for a right-wing Final Solution. I would have thought that the claims were so ludicrous that no one could possibly take them seriously, but the phones haven't stopped ringing. 'Why do you kill gays?' 'Are you unusual, or are all Australians violent fuckin' homophobes?' 'Did your daddy wupp you when you wuz a boy?' (Definitely not whipped, *wupped*!) 'Are you a latent homosexual?' I wanted to answer that I am a closet heterosexual, but the headline would write itself, KILLER FUCKS VICTIMS IN CLOSET.[11] When the Council decided against having an anonymous Killer, it hoped that everything would be up-front, that their openness would counteract innuendo and rumour of this kind. Now I find that having made no secret of my identity, I have a dozen new secret identities fabricated for me every week. If I were to open an autobiographical volume with the line, 'My parents brought me up on a diet of human flesh . . .' (a show-stopper of an opening line, admittedly) half the population of the planet would turn to

---

11 These observations provoked extended debate at the Elliot Commission, with at least three psychiatrists prepared to argue the case for overstrenuous (Freudian) denial, suggesting that Thompson was precisely what he was denying himself to be, a latent homosexual and a homophobe. Witherspoon later rejected this as a 'convoluted attempt to establish a psychopathology for Thompson which has no basis in hard evidence'.

their friends and say, 'There, I told you so. It was obvious all along that he was a cannibal.' The more truthful you try to be, the more people will suspect that you are concealing something.

* * *

Maybe there is only a finite number of gazes or perceptual dispositions, sixteen or eighteen, like camera settings, and all your thoughts, memories, and perceptions are connected by these possible ways of experiencing the world.

* * *

They sicken me, the Virginia Woolfs and Kafkas who kept the most exquisite, closely observed journals for years. Never a weak sentence. A succession of astute, microscopic observations to complement a mastery of tone and narrative situation. In their journals, even the most mundane predicament was full of possibility and insinuation. Here I am, an authorised killer, a man who has ended the lives of more than thirty individuals, and yet I would be incapable of describing just what it is that I do, even if discretion allowed me to. I can say nothing, do nothing, write nothing, think nothing that places my methods at risk. Yet a Woolf or a Kafka faced with the same limitations would still find a way to say what is essential. They'd create a metaphoric world. You would know from the unsaid, the scrupulously chosen verbs, tenses, and clauses, what it is to exercise a unique sanction, to be the banal face of horror, to be a repossession man. Every night, they would compose a string of perfect sentences, assembling the ingredients that would one day become a perfect work of art. For whom does a diarist write? Do I write for myself, thirty years hence, a jaded ex-killer retired to a country estate in Ireland? Do I address myself to the burglar who hopes to sell this diary to a German magazine? Or do I speak to something much more abstract, Posterity? I write because I want to explore the limits of what I can and can't write, to find a way beyond the prohibitions and limitations that come with being a living legend made legendary by death.

* * *

Favourite Foods (as requested by *The Hampton Bugle*)
Sushi
Fried eggs on (burnt-ish) buttered toast
Muesli (with yoghurt)
Crisp roast duckling in plum sauce
Swiss chocolate, and Belgian chocolate truffles
Grilled barramundi
Jelly babies, snakes, killer pythons, milk bottles etc
Mushroom risotto
Steamed broccoli
Bacon and avocado bagels

* * *

In the past week, I've received 246 items of mail. That's a little more than average, but correspondence tends to increase as the Festival approaches. At least two-thirds of it is requests for autographs or photographs. Generally, there will be four or five requests for a souvenir from one of the Martyrs. There are invitations to openings, to private parties, approaches for product endorsements, and party political endorsements, and requests for charitable appearances: fete openings, hospital visits, even 'Could you sing at our karaoke night?' (What do you think, the Talking Heads' number 'Psycho Killer'? There was a request to appear in a charity cricket match for cancer research, 'Husbands versus Bachelors' . . . The World Wildlife Fund wanted to know whether I could help out in any way with their new Giant Panda breeding program. I'm not so sure that their efforts on behalf of the endangered species of the world would necessarily benefit from an association with a notorious hired killer. Still, I sent them a poem I wrote while I was at high school.

The Black and White Rag

All the forms of propaganda
Fashion a world
That's black and white
Just like a panda.
(And who doesn't like a panda?)

Those monochromes of cuddly cute
Spend their days on bamboo chutes
Until the last bamboo's been shot
And pandas can curl up in the cot
Just like a cuddly toy.
(And who doesn't like a cuddly toy?)[12]

I get bundles of mail from women saying that they want to sleep with me, that God has predetermined that we should sleep together. Letters from women saying that they want to save me. (Presumably by

---

12 The World Wildlife Fund denied having received this poem. Thompson was notoriously slow in dealing with correspondence. WWF now intend to use the poem in campaign advertising.

sleeping with me.) Every week for the past two years, one young man from Auckland has sent me a sealed plastic bag containing his semen. Well, I assume that the semen is his. He and his friends may take a collection . . .[13] This week, I received seven death threats, four copies of the Bible, and an album of photos taken in Belsen immediately after the liberation. I am being prayed for. I have been told to be wary of a French-speaking assassin hired by the Vatican. One father wrote that he would be grateful if I could take on his fifteen-year-old son for work experience. 'He is strong, discreet, and very thorough.' (Perhaps I should recommend him to my Auckland correspondent!) I am always receiving gratuitous psychiatric advice—I should tell them that my desire to kill is all a consequence of my daddy having 'wupped' me when I was a boy. It wouldn't annoy me so much if these psychiatrists were asking for information so that they might learn from my experiences. (One Indian doctor did ask me whether I'd ever had 'an unwarranted erection' while strangling or smothering a victim? What on earth does an *unwarranted* erection look like, and how could an erection be 'warranted' in those circumstances?) Mostly, I'm assailed with learnedness, surmise, and arrogance. What you *really* want is . . . Not that all the experts disagree with my chosen profession. Dr Stella Bronowski of Maryland tells me that she has nearly completed her study *Killing as Catharsis* . . . On the one hand, I am a model citizen, on the other, I am a model psychopath . . . I am asked

---

13 In her testimony before the Elliot Commission, Thompson's personal secretary, Astrid de Groot, denied having seen these semen donations. She was later charged with conspiring to murder Thompson.

to help with homework projects in Budapest. I receive suggested methods for future killings—some of them remarkably ingenious. I receive recipes for cakes and casseroles, business propositions, a dozen outright begging letters. Sometimes I feel like I have my head stuck through the centre of a target, and that I'm being pounded with wet sponges . . . 'If you don't mind me saying so, I think that you should dress better. Blacks and whites make you look so pallid and drained. You need bright colours.'

* * *

I should write this book. I've been sleepwalking for too long. A disorganised pursuit like journal-writing fails to clarify things. You pose the question, and then avoid the difficulty of trying to answer it. A structure would force me to attend to the matters I have avoided in these pages . . . Why did I back out of killing X? Was it, as I persuaded myself, that there would be no opportune moment (when my job is to contrive and manufacture opportune moments), or was it cowardice: that I feared the consequences? A dutiful Killer has to be prepared to die in carrying out the duties of the office. It's one thing to rationalise my position by saying that I am under constant threat from enemies, assassins, and psychopaths, I have a duty to defend the integrity of my position. Not all threats are overt. The public is told that my parents and family live outside of Hampton because I cannot be compromised in terms of my choice of victim. The public has not been told that my family lives in exile, with changed appearances and identities, in order to save my office from the threat of blackmail by organised crime. I believe in the Festival, and I believe in the importance of my agency, but in ideal

94

terms Hampton is only the barest approximation of the
Utopian society that it presents to the public gaze. Only
the most naive person subscribes to the notion of
absolute purity, that you can dissociate yourself entirely
from the vast, corrupt forces that surround you, that
you can build a Utopian civilisation on an island in the
middle of a cesspit.[14] Every reality is a flawed approximation of the ideas that brought it into being. I like the
notion of approximation. To approximate is to assert
your inability to arrive at the Truth. You fashion a poetry
that hovers in the vicinity of the truth. I remember
the director Louis Malle speaking of film-making as a
sequence of broad approximations that are gradually
refined, and then brought into the concentrated focus
of a central narrative. But identity's not like that. The
only time identity is like that is when it takes the form
of the false identity celebrated in autobiography. In
reality, you can't assemble identity like a film, eliminat-
ing entire scenes and performances, pretending that
what has been cut, whether it be one frame or five
hundred, never existed. Identity is messier than ortho-
dox documentary can allow for. Only in fiction do you
get the most accurate approximations of true identity.
If I were to write my autobiography most truthfully, it
would need to take the form of an expressionistic
fiction. Just as Kafka places his clerks in overwhelming
situations that indicate their true relation to the
cosmos, I would need to discover or unveil the essence
of my identity by presenting myself as a man who
imagines that he has been hired to kill seven residents

---

14 Along with many readers, I find this remark so staggeringly
ironic that it is difficult to imagine Thompson made it
innocently. Dr Pamela Woodland asked, 'Is it possible for a
remark to be too innocent to be innocent?'

of a suburb every year.[15] To simply proclaim that you are, in reality, just such a killer is immediately delimiting. It brings to mind something that Borges wrote, that all classification implies falsification. Classification smooths over difference and contradiction. Being the Killer is not my identity, it isn't what I am, it is something that I am at once moving towards and away from in a kind of elliptical orbit. I am an array of possibilities that can't necessarily be expressed by, or embraced by, what I do or what I've done. I like the line in one of Hal Hartley's films, 'I'm bad at my job on purpose. If I was any better at it, I might become what I do for a living.'[16] Killing people for a good reason—to sustain a community—is not nearly so odious as being identified as the Killer.

* * *

A series of wrong numbers, all pathetic types asking 'Is that Leggy ex-Model?' 'Mate, do I *sound* like a leggy ex-model?' There must have been a misprinted phone number in an ad for Adult Services. I find it fascinating to imagine the kind of man who could get fired-up at the thought of someone so indefinite as 'Leggy ex-Model'. (Why did she retire? Just how ex is ex, and what exactly did she model?) People often ask what frightens

---

15 These meditations were the source of prolonged debate before both Elliot and Witherspoon. On the one hand, Thompson's self-conscious manipulation of identity was seen as connivance, to throw up screens of irony and hyper self-awareness. On the other, the passage was interpreted as an innocent attempt by a man in the throes of an identity crisis to determine who he is, and what he might become. Witherspoon observed that Thompson, in his pursuit of personal truths, sometimes muddied *the* truth. He argued that it is Thompson's very honesty that makes him so exceptionally unreliable.

16 The Hartley film alluded to is *The Theory of Achievement*.

me most, and I can never find a good answer at the time. I must remember to mention phrases with numbers in them; 'the wrong number', 'Your number is up' . . . I don't know why, but they chill me. And this was well before I became Fate's bingo caller. Something about numbers. A friend once told me that there are villages in Africa where they don't have streets or streetnames, and the houses aren't numbered according to their location or physical proximity, but according to when they were built. So you are looking for someone who lives in 127, and you know that it was the house that was built after 126, but it might be nowhere near 126, way on the other side of town, nestled between 5 and 37. The locals aren't the slightest bit fazed by this. They read Kafka for the jokes. (Did I ever mention that I bought my personal computer from a salesman whose name appeared on the docket as 'Joseph K.'? Franz has gone hi-tech.) After learning about these numbered villages, I had disturbed sleep for weeks. 'Mate, we have your number.' 'Richard Thompson, your days are numbered.'

* * *

'*Warning! Warning! Danger, Will Robinson!*' . . . Daphne Emerson from Amnesty International called to advise me that the Hampton Festival of Killing would be the subject of a television documentary co-produced by Amnesty and Channel 4. Their choice of Christine Marker as writer–director is surprising. Though she has been a vocal critic of military dictatorships in South-East Asia and the Americas, as a rule she writes quirky short stories. I read one of Christine Marker's collections, *Days Without Violence*, and I wouldn't be surprised if she regards this documentary as research for a future novel. Of course, the involvement of Amnesty makes the film's slant predictable. (I should purchase a pair of plastic vampire fangs.) As always in these affairs, if you choose not to participate, you'll be shot down from a distance (like a member of the Royal Family). On the other hand, you can offer to speak to them and be shot down at close range. A skilled film-maker can edit anything to support a thesis. If, for example, while being filmed, I chose to justify my actions by using an argument I've used previously (and persuasively), they would collage all previous versions of the statement to indicate that my argument is too well rehearsed, therefore dubious or insincere. It would not be in the film-maker's interests to show that I am well liked and admired. Still, I have a politician's ego, and I enjoy making claims for the importance of my office. What's more, I look forward to meeting Christine Marker. I could ask her to sign my copy of her book. If the photo on the back cover is anything to go by, Christine's a very attractive woman. She looks a little like Francesca . . . I suppose that it's inevitable that she will ask me to remember Francesca.[17]

* * *

When I said I was warned that I *would* be the subject of the Channel 4/Amnesty documentary, I had it

---

17 Francesca Morricone, a former intimate of Thompson, disappeared while travelling in Denmark and was presumed murdered. Francesca later appeared before Witherspoon, to claim that she had faked her disappearance before taking up residence in London. She saw this strategy as her means of breaking with the obsessed Thompson. She said that Thompson had ignored her previous attempts to terminate their friendship. Morricone's surprise testimony before the Witherspoon Commission discredited an earlier attempt to link Francesca's disappearance with that of Christine Marker.

wrong. It seems that I *am* the subject of a documentary. The producers have already researched old friends who live outside of Hampton. Tracey called last night to tell me that she would be speaking to them. I told her that I supposed she would relish the opportunity to drop another bucket on me. When she said, 'No, but I'll answer their questions truthfully' I felt like asking what she—of all people—would know of the truth. I resisted. Tracey's quite capable of wounding me without provoking her further.

* * *

To judge from the things said and written about me, I am most admired for my decisiveness. People want to believe that I am an active, assertive person. The converse is closer to the truth. I believe that I was chosen to be the Killer because I was understood to be a compliant, anxious person who would choose to honour his commitment to his employer, even if a conflict of interest arose. Killing is no job for the impulsive or reckless. Far from being a law unto himself, the Killer's actions are more regulated, more scrutinised than any other member of this society. I have power only in so far as I am empowered. (I think that I should begin to practise the minimalist waves and hand gestures favoured by the Royal Family.)[18]

* * *

I remember Mrs Dallas, my English teacher at Hampton High, taking offence at a story I wrote about the staff's involvement with Satanism, arguing that it is possible

---

18 For the second time in three entries, Thompson draws a link between himself and royalty, lending weight to the view that the Killer unconsciously adopted the mind-set of an aristocrat.

to have too much imagination . . . She said that, while it's proper to venerate the Shakespeares and Tolstoys, it's also worth remembering that the people who do the most terrible things are often the people with the most fertile imaginations—'There are times when you'll need to reign in your fantasies.' Though I take Mrs D.'s point, I can also see that there is a paradoxical aspect to what she was saying. I'm not sure whether it takes a stupendous imagination or a feeble one to imagine that you could live at peace, or be happy, after performing a terrible premeditated act. When John Hinckley Jr thought that he could win Jodie Foster's heart by assassinating President Reagan, was Hinckley's imagination depleted or over-charged? (Could a person accept the task of killing seven individuals a year purely to impress former girlfriends, or to stick it up the people who said that he'd never amount to anything?) And you can apply this paradox of imagination to the larger-scale Utopian dreams. Was the Soviet Union— born from the notion that you could realise a happy, truly egalitarian society (from accepting the fallacious belief that a political system can disregard or change fundamental human impulses)—a consequence of too little imagination, or too much imagination? From experience, I can split the critics of Hampton's Festival into two, roughly equal camps. There are those who insist that the Festival, and the Hampton community shaped by the Festival, is an anti-Christian, socialist abomination. And there are just as many critics who argue that the Festival is a predictable development in the brutish history of capitalism. I can only say that I wouldn't kill anyone if the people of Hampton didn't wish me to kill. And someone else would surely do it if I didn't. I do know that I haven't the imagination to picture a world where an absolute moral code pertains, a world free of mists or patches of grey.

* * *

King of the kids. I'd no sooner finished officiating at the opening of the new child care centre, than I was at the primary school being introduced to a class of six and seven-year-olds. As good fortune had it, I hadn't killed any of their parents. Most of the children had been doing projects on the Killer for the past fortnight. One boy was under something of a misapprehension, clearly fuelled by his father. 'Why did you kill my rabbit? . . . My dad said that you came to kill my rabbit because we couldn't have a dog and a rabbit.' The teacher tried to help out. 'Mr Thompson's a very kind man, Danny. He never kills animals.' 'But he *killed* Thaddeus! He broke his neck!' After a while, Mrs Ingstrom managed to persuade Danny that I hadn't killed Thaddeus. The problem was that he knew *someone* had wasted his bunny, and the idea that the Killer isn't responsible for all killings is confusing to a kid who still harbours the view that Santa is responsible for all Christmas presents. During question time, a lot of them wanted to be individually reassured that I wouldn't harm their pets. (Their parents they couldn't have cared less about . . . Once a kid made me promise that I wouldn't kill Bart and Lisa Simpson.) They tend to ask the same questions: Have you ever buried anyone alive? Do you ever eat people after you kill them? Have you ever met Batman and Superman? Couldn't you just blow up a bus and take five years holiday? What subjects do you have to be good at in school to become the Killer? Does your mum know you kill people? Did your parents tell you that killing people was wrong when you were a

kid? Do you ever just hurt people and not kill them? . . .
We sat in the same classroom where I was taught by Miss
Hogan in grade one. Back then we didn't seem to worry
so much. During recess, the boys played War, America
versus the Germans. (Never Australia versus the Japanese.) They've replaced the old blackboards with
whiteboards, and the big television room—where the
entire school crammed in to watch Armstrong walk on
the moon—has become the computer room. The old
desks have gone, but there's a smell that never goes
away, the smell of sawdust over vomit. Which brings to
mind my favourite question: Do you clean up after you
kill someone, or does your mum do it for you?

* * *

Why do I deny things, choose the most pessimistic
interpretation? Even to the extent that I was reluctant
to report here what Christine had said for fear that I'd
misread her meaning. It happened while I was stating
the terms and conditions for filming in the house. 'I'd
love to know what your bedroom looks like,' Christine
had said. Ordinarily, I would have laughed off such
obvious innuendo, but my extreme guardedness in this
instance must have been unmistakable to her. I am a
person who over-reads, who feels assailed by a barrage
of possible subtexts.[19] I choose to determine, immediately, seriously, that what she actually means is that a
person's most private room reveals a lot about their

---

19 Several expert witnesses who testified before Elliot and
  Witherspoon interpreted these utterances as a specific invitation
  to read the journal for its subtexts and allusions. According to
  this analysis, Thompson was producing a calculated text that
  would mask or confuse his real (criminal) motives. Witherspoon
  demurred, stating that the passage only indicated that Thompson
  was preoccupied with self-analysis to the point of obsession.

true nature, and that the Killer's bedroom would be of special interest. Is he messy or meticulous? Sloppy or obsessive? Why do I not want to believe the possibility that Christine may be expressing—albeit in a public, jokified form—a desire to become more intimately acquainted with the bedroom's resident? Why are my desires so terrifying? I have always been overwhelmed by the strength of my desires, and will do everything within my power to suppress them, seeing any hope of their realisation as a cruel trick played by an overactive imagination. If only there was a way to cut through the poetry and inexactness of human communication, to ascertain what was meant, exactly. (We killers are so fond of final arbitrations—The Definite)

* * *

It must be difficult to be a man. To be firm and decisive, to always know exactly what you want and be single-minded in the pursuit of it; to be inflamed by fragrances and suggested curves, willing to betray anyone or anything—family, sacred beliefs and ideals—for just a few minutes with your dick inside something wet and womanly; to be as one with other men, part beast yet authoritative; to be always testing the boundaries of violation; to be able to presume that the magic wand in your trousers will be the final persuasion, that its potent maleness will necessarily do someone a favour; to firmly believe that you know what a woman wants, to know what she needs, and to know how to withhold feeling and emotion until that moment when your sex can be revealed like a rabbit hidden up a sleeve; to be a man able to divide women into two groups: those to be disregarded except for their labours, and those who deserve to be fucked, and to define yourself by your ticked-off conquests, by your capacity to aggress; to aggressively initiate and fulfil the manly functions, and to exclude any woman who would threaten that capacity or question its worth; to be powerfully unpredictable, predictably powerful, cocksure yet wary, wary of women; to be on a collision course with your wariness of women; to bluff until you believe in your own bluff. The difficulty of inhabiting a mad, pinball reality, a pinball sexuality. So much easier to be a Killer.

* * *

I'm convinced that there are two types of people in the world. There are the people who want to know how the television works, and the people who don't want to know. The people who don't want to know aren't bothered that laws, rules, structures and explanations exist. They might even find it consoling to know that the things they don't want to know *can* be known. It's just that the people who don't want to know relish the *idea* of magic, the idea that television exists as pure wonderment. They want to believe in magical forces, and miraculous fusions and inspirations. Scientific knowledge is too rational, too available, too democratic. They need a magician.

* * *

After hearing rumours that the producer of the Amnesty/Channel 4 documentary intends to use 'docudrama recreations' of specific killings, I called Lorraine di, telling her that she should make it known to them that any unauthorised dramatisation of a killing would violate The Festival Act, and would necessitate legal action. Though Lorraine was very aware of how such a 'factional' presentation might misrepresent or damage the Festival, she pointed out that any legal threats that we made could only be bluff. If Hampton went to court to point out the discrepancies between the documentary's dramatic recreations of specific killings and the circumstances of those killings, it would be forced to make public information germane to gambling interests . . . How would it ever be possible to tell the truth of what I do when so many conflicting interests govern and appropriate my actions? The most truthful dramatic recreation of Hampton's Killer would depict him as a plasticine figure, a Gumby, artfully shaped and reshaped for every circumstance.

* * *

Once again, I've been voted one of the ten worst dressed men in Australia. What can I do? I used to like the jackets and windcheaters with the 'K' insignia, but then the Tourist Commission began to market them on a large scale, and it seemed tacky for the tourist attraction to dress like the tourists. Of course, the people at the bureau would be delighted if I wore a black, hooded cloak, and carried a scythe. The postcard sales would go through the roof. I spent most of one year in a very elegant black suit—'People don't come all this way to have their photo taken with a bank manager!' Now, in jeans, and sneakers, and t-shirt, I'm a dag, I'm an international fashion disaster. I know I shouldn't be so sensitive about it, but I've always had a neurotic desire to please everyone. The next time I see someone described as 'dressed to kill', I'm going to drop the biggest bucket. Why aren't these people who are supposedly 'dressed to kill' dressed like me?—Maybe attack is the best form of defence. I could recommend a

Fashion is Murder Week to the Council, or dash off a coffee table volume, *Dressing to Kill*, full of comfortable après-homicide wear. It might make a nice change, to be able to speak as an authority.

* * *

I dream that I am walking rapidly along a narrow laneway, defined on either side by tall hedging. The sensation is that of being confined in a maze, though I can see a tiny opening in the distance. Yet my progress seems to take me no closer to that opening. I am anxious, always looking back over my shoulder. Behind me, the two rows of hedge meet at the horizon. I can hear a roaring noise in the distance which may be the sea. Other than that, there is only the sky to suggest a world beyond the corridor of hedge. As I run and stumble towards the ever-distant opening, I begin to repeat the same word, a confusion between breathing and voice, a word like 'instrument', or perhaps, 'experiment'. Whatever the word, it seems to me that I am uttering a secret shame, a taboo.[20]

* * *

S. says that I'm the Killer because I lacked the discipline to learn a musical instrument, that being a guitar hero would've given me a better opportunity to

---

20 'A heavy-handed plant' in the opinion of forensic psychiatrist Professor Nigel Browne in his testimony before Witherspoon. Browne argued that the account of this dream suggests an author who knows enough about dream theory and analysis to remain ambiguous, but not enough to be subtle. According to Professor Browne, 'the dream smacks of cynical contrivance', though Browne was reluctant to speculate on Thompson's possible motives.

express whatever it is that I need to express. As much as I love music, I'm no musician. I'm a singer with no range. The Killer doesn't have to be brilliant night after night. He can hit as many false notes as he likes, he can be as flatulent as he likes, so long as he is efficient the seven times when his efficiency is required. He chooses his moment. As a twelve or thirteen-year-old, I would've killed to be Cat Stevens, or Ian Anderson, or Robert Plant (And if they'd killed to be me, they would've *been* me . . .) Christine tells me that she wanted to become a singer, but her father forbade it.[21] She was sent to an art school in London to study graphic design, but she knew that she wanted to write and make films. She laughs when I tell her that she looks different to the author photo on the back of *Days Without Violence*. 'Older and less attractive,' she suggests. I don't know what it is about her that makes me think of Francesca, but I warm to her as someone that I know, and trust, rather than the interviewer whose task is to character-assassinate me. I would speak of her more in terms of loveliness than beauty. When she finishes laughing, she beams, her broad smile gradually dissipating. (Who was that KAOS agent in *Get Smart*? Melvic the Smiling Killer . . . I will need to watch Christine—when I am not too busy looking at her!) She is not particularly dictatorial with

---

21 This exchange may have taken place during a non-transcripted interview in late-October. Many of Thompson's earlier journals are time-specific, and the absence of dates in this volume aroused scepticism. The Hampton Coroner Helen O'Brien regarded the lack of exact dates as evidence of a possible inauthenticity. She argued that Thompson's time-imprecision is convenient in that it neutralises the possibility of factual contradiction, and does not allow us to speculate on the context in which a particular entry may have been written. Several witnesses expressed surprise that Thompson found time to write at such length.

her crew. Her cameraman Michael tends to dominate the arrangement of things. I made it clear to him that I was unwilling to take part in a stylised documentary, that the crew would have to situate themselves to suit me. It's much too easy for a skilled practitioner to make you look like an imbecile with their low-angles and wide angles and fish-eyes. (They'll manage to do this anyway, but that doesn't mean that I shouldn't try to circumvent or obstruct their strategies.) I can see that they intend a game of cat and mouse, that the most confronting questions will be withheld till they feel that I am off guard or vulnerable. Hence this game of flattery and counter-flattery. The camera pans along my bookshelves, examines the titles in my video collection, the framed Munch print on the wall, the undried dishes in the rack on the sink. *Do you have any photographs of your parents or family?* Not for the camera. *Do you keep photographs of your victims?* No. But there are many photographs of them in the Shrine. *Can we film you there?* No . . . Christine is surprised that I have read her stories, but I am disinclined to let her know what I think of her work before she has given some indication of the slant of her documentary. I'm surprised to find that she speaks English like a speech and drama teacher yet a second party has been credited with translating *Days Without Violence* from the original French.[22] She *could* have been a singer, I think. There is a melody in her voice. Perhaps she is hoping that I will reveal that money is my uppermost concern. Or, she would like me to think that this is

---

22 On the title page of *Days Without Violence*, credit for the English translation is attributed to Carlotta Valdes, though it is highly likely that Carlotta Valdes is a pseudonym adopted by Marker when translating her own text.

her angle, that I am to be portrayed as a simple mercenary. I will credit her researchers with having more perception than that.

* * *

You fumble along, hoping that what you do does more good than harm. Hampton's Killer doesn't know his final place in history any more than Richard Nixon does. Or Margaret Thatcher, or Bob Hawke. As much as you'd like to protest the fact, you're a gambler. (Hold onto your tickets, there's a protest in the Posterity Handicap: second-placed Killer versus the winning favourite, Wisdom of Hindsight.) The very last thing I expected when I took on the job was that I'd become the Prince of Punt. No one in my family ever gambled. It wasn't that the Thompsons were particularly wowser-ish or frugal. I was brought up to believe that the only money that meant anything, the only money worth having, was the money derived from honest toil—the old fashioned values of the WASP middle class. Back in the sixties, as I was growing up, there was nothing glamorous about gambling. Gambling seemed to be the last refuge of the lowly and desperate. For me, gambling was the horses, and the unshaven men who sat up at their laminex tables on Saturday arvo, ears glued to the fourth from Caulfield, making pen-marks on sheets of hieroglyphed newspaper, and pouring glasses of beer from brown bottles. Gambling and alcoholism were inextricably linked in my imagination, a sad con-junction of too hopeful hopelessness. This jaundiced view would have been formed by the bottle-drives. When I was a kid in scouts, the local scout troop used to raise money by collecting bottles. You'd dash around Hampton carting hessian bags full of clinking bottles out to utes, or cars with trailers. We were little kids in scarves and baggy shorts sifting through tall stacks of brown bottles, all covered in webs, and snails, and slaters. The unshaven man with the Caulfield races blaring from his transistor directed you behind his shed or garage to a mountain of alcoholic refuse. By the end of the day, the scum dribbling through the hessian bags left your scout uniform stinking of stale beer. We were innocent intruders, confident that we were doing these unshaven men a favour, quite unaware that we had access to saleable information. We could have compiled an alcoholic map of Hampton and sold it off to employers and insurers for a lot more than we ever got for the glass. Insurance companies would have paid a fortune for a detailed map of Hampton's alcoholics. That culture, the heavy drinking and the gambling, was foreign to my experience at home, and I looked down on those people. Open expression of moral superiority was socially acceptable in the sixties. Now, your moral judgements have to be carefully concealed within statements about diet, fitness, and health. If you'd told me in the 1960s that the status of gambling would have been elevated to a form of civic duty, that gambling would one day form the economic foundation of this society, I wouldn't have believed it possible. It would have been like accepting that you'd have to bathe in a trough of stale beer every Saturday for the rest of your life . . . I dunno. Is it possible to be a fatalist and not believe in luck? I'm not sure that I understand what luck is. Is bad luck finding yourself next in line for Martyrdom, or last in line? Was it only good luck that the bouncer's arm came down behind my back to signal a full house when The Cure played the tiny Armadale Hotel in 1980? The arm had to come down somewhere.

In the general run of things, you are lucky because you are not unlucky. Take that poor bloke in the newspaper (urban myth disguised as news?): the Greek scuba diver found burnt to death in a forest fire. There he is, just minding his own business, swimming a metre deep in the blue sea, when a helicopter—or was it some sort of water plane?—picks him up in a water scoop and dumps him on a forest fire. I mean, what happens inside the poor bastard's head? Is he thinking, My number, my number is up? He's trapped up there with all that water and fish and seaweed and shit. Is Barber's *Adagio for Strings* playing on his personal soundtrack? If it's luck, it's a filthy bit of luck. Totally fucked. But I don't see how you can *ride* luck, or *make* your own luck, or that certain individuals are graced in terms of luck. You could be like George Zanotti, the guy who won a couple of million betting that a male between 20 and 30 would be the next Hamptonian martyred the week before David Miller was killed. Is George lucky because he had an instance of good luck, because he won a fortune he didn't earn? Is he lucky because of his stars, or because he touched a Chinaman? Or is he lucky because he experienced the *absence* of bad luck, because he didn't fall off the ladder and become quadriplegic, because he didn't become charcoal inside his wetsuit? This is a hopeless fucking world of might and maybe and possible and probable . . . On Tuesday, it will be two years since Jenny Fitzpatrick died. She was 28 or 29, and she had a massive brain haemorrhage. What Jenny never knew was that she was so nearly the fourth Martyr. Had she been killed, she might have been Hampton's last Martyr. It was a very near thing. To all intents and purposes, Jenny looked like a normal girl. Her family believed that she was normal, and never accepted that the brain

111

injuries she'd copped in a cycling accident had left her intellectually bereft. Maybe they ought to have signed documents to have Jenny exempted from the social contract, but they didn't, and not because they thought her dispensable. They didn't want people to regard her as deficient or different. They wanted her to be accepted as a full member of the community. Jenny would accompany her father to his office, sit at a desk opposite his, receive a full salary, and present like the elegant young solicitor that I'd been given to believe that she was. Was it a stroke of luck that a friend told me an anecdote about the local solicitor and his vacant mascot the day before Jenny was to be martyred? That would have been the end of the Festival. You can imagine the outcry about euthanasia and eugenics and final solutions. The thought of it still chills me. Lucky? Who can say whether Jenny was lucky to have had those three extra years? Or whether Christine Nelson, (who then became the fourth Martyr) was uncommonly unlucky? . . . You just fumble along, hoping that what you do does more good than harm, needing to believe it, but would you want to bet your life on it?

* * *

I've been thinking of Christine. She left a lipstick impression on one of my coffee mugs, and I can't bring myself to clean it off. In my thoughts of her, I find it difficult to separate her from Francesca, yet I may be the only person in the world to see this likeness. I am unable to articulate the nature of the similarity (can a person be said to have a tone or ambience?) or the reason for my inclination to see this similarity. I'm surprised to find I have a powerful desire for Christine, because she is quite removed from my favoured physical type. I'm also frightened by what my friends and former friends may have said to her. Of course, I expect Tracey to tell her that I am impotent and pathetic. I can wear that. But what if she speaks to Catherine?[23] What if Catherine should tell the world what she never found the courage to tell me to my face: that she never had any powerful or intimate feeling for me, that my strange sense of involvement/intimacy with her was just extravagant fantasy? As a perceptive writer, Christine will see that I have a habit of fixation. She will predict the likelihood that I will become obsessed with her, and will use artful seduction to draw me into revelations which may damage myself or my office. I don't doubt that she despises my profession. I will need to be contrary to her expectations, to anticipate her moves, and to surprise. She may be Catholic. She may have an overriding desire to have me renounce my work on film. Her position may turn out to be as vulnerable as my own.

* * *

It feels good to be scheming again, to lose myself in the arrangements for the next dispensation. Once the wheels are set in motion, I become totally immersed in the details, all the things that need to be attended to. People will tell me that I am distracted, far away. It is this immersal that I relish. Suddenly the world seems to be still and quiet, and I can shift the pieces back and forth as I choose. Unlike the political assassin, the Killer

23 Catherine O'Shaunessy was one of Thompson's long-term obsessions, pre-dating his term as Hampton's Killer. Like Francesca Morricone, O'Shaunessy tired of Richard Thompson's fixation, and broke off their friendship. Ironically, she also ended up living in London, less than 500 metres from Francesca. She is now a Professor of Forensic Pathology at the City University.

has no need to get caught up in motives or emotions . . . When I started, I thought that it would be best if I took on the mind-set of a robot or automaton, but I discovered, paradoxically, that it's humanity that makes the program possible. Humanity and intuition enable me to anticipate irregularities and caprice. I told an interviewer once that the Killer needs to be a poet. You are not dealing with method, or the logic of progression, so much as the logic of dance. To be part of the dance, you have to make yourself inseparable from the rhythm, embracing the subtle shifts of density, the distance between sounds. When you have planned, plotted, and rehearsed to the extent that you can give yourself over to irrational forces, the Martyr will choose him or herself. You begin to see the Martyr beckoning you. When I am scheming, a power surges through me so that I never doubt that what I am doing is of the utmost importance, that I am a traffic policeman at the crossroads of history. My identity and my actions are as one. I was wrong in my attitude to the Hartley quote. I do my job well precisely because I *hope to* become what I do. I swell. I extend. I surpass myself.

* * *

Wherever you go, you see the essential wisdom of Hitchcock's *Vertigo*: desire fashions reality. We need the truth to be that particular arrangement of facts that most readily conforms to our understanding of what the truth *should* be or has to be. To those who need the Killer to be a flawless hero, he is faultless, exemplary. To those who reject the Killer's function, he is someone who lives in perpetual shade, a shadowy Michael Jackson figure.

* * *

I was half hoping to see Jane again today, trying to concoct an accidental meeting. (Most days she eats lunch at The Deli.) As I walked up Hampton Street, I got caught in a sudden hailstorm, and had to take refuge under the veranda at the Tourist Bureau just as a busload of visitors pulled in. Half-soaked, miserable as hell, I was bombarded with camera flashes and requests for signatures. 'I don't believe it,' one old duck enthused, 'The Harbour Bridge, Uluru, and the Barrier Reef . . . now the Killer.' I'd like to bet that none of the other attractions signed autographs, though it would make for quite a slide night back home. This is a photograph of Uluru, pissed-off at getting caught in a hailstorm . . . One man from Florida must have anticipated this irregular meeting, and offered me a present that he'd brought to Hampton specially to give to the Killer. 'It's something that I think you should have,' he tells me as I unwrap a speargun. 'My sister killed my daddy with it.' Sometimes I feel as though I possess more murder weapons than the IRA, or the Mau Mau. I thanked the man, and told him that he should drop me a letter detailing his sister's speargun escapade, in case I'm required to donate the weapon to a museum at some stage in the future.

* * *

An invitation to S.'s fancy dress party—COME AS YOUR FAVOURITE FICTIONAL CHARACTER. I'm very tempted to go as Humpty Dumpty. For me, Humpty signifies the fragility of knowledge, the inevitability of subversion, and the problem of continuous identity. If H.D. could be pieced together again, would he still be an egg? Can any of our actions or our errors be entirely undone? . . . If I can get a costume, I might go as Bullwinkle the Moose. The thing is, Bullwinkle isn't so much a favourite fictional character as he is a role model. Bullwinkle is fabulously stoic. He's feckless but imperturbable. When confronted with the consequences of his ignorance or misplaced confidence, Bullwinkle is ever-resilient, always finding the courage to forge onwards. Rosi Braidotti once said of Sartre that he had the courage of his contradictions, and Bullwinkle has that in buckets. It's the best sort of courage, I think, the undaunted commitment to commitment for its own sake. When Rocky's voice of reason tells Bullwinkle, 'that trick will never work', Bullwinkle doesn't even pause to consider the possibility of failure, 'This time for sure!'

* * *

Still more requests to prepare an autobiography, or to assist an authorised biography . . . I don't know. I feel as if I've begun to stalk myself. I'm constricted by too much consciousness of who I am, and what I am doing. The exercise could liberate me, or it could undo me entirely. Last night, I began to look at Francesca's letters. I hadn't even considered reading them since they were returned by the police. And they are still too painful, the way that she would double-guess me, and take the piss out of my so-obsessive letter writing. The first one I opened was her *Ten Year Prospectus of Richard's Letters to Francesca* . . .

July 10, 2003: Will write to Francesca to complain that she has not written since May. Will point out one or two recent political happenings. Will tell a funny (perhaps invented) tale about a brush-tail possum . . . July 14, 2003: Will complain to Francesca that her letter of July 8 did not tackle the matters raised in my letter of July 3. Will make one or two banal observations about the Melbourne winter. Will assert the absolute truth of a previously told story about an eccentric film society based in a (fabricated) Melbourne cafe, Travis Bickle's.[24]

Francesca's letters destroy me. I can't imagine reading them again without pain, nor can I imagine releasing them for the perusal of a biographer. But to rid myself of them, to actually destroy them, would be to initiate something more profoundly destructive.

* * *

How will Christine pursue the Francesca connection? She has a writer's perceptions and intuitions. What if she should discover more than I already know myself?

* * *

I was woken at five this morning by a phenomenal roll of thunder, and was unable to return to sleep. Very black thoughts. I've been plagued by the notion that I have chased off or alienated everyone that I have loved, that I have chosen a path which will inevitably alienate them. I couldn't even settle to read anything, not even to re-read old favourites like Swift and Gogol. Picked out Machiavelli, but never even opened it, my mind immediately racing off to the furious argument

---

24 Francesca Morricone destroyed most of the letters she received from Thompson, and no evidence of this letter remains.

that I had about *The Prince* with Yuri on Oslo Railway Station.[25] Yuri insisted that a non-smoker should always carry a cigarette lighter in order to maximise his chances of meeting women. I could scarcely imagine anything more transparently immoral. (Immorally transparent?) Yuri always considered Machiavelli to be an *advocate* of 'end justifies the means' transactions. I prefer to see Machiavelli as a bemused analyst of historical realities. If I were 'accused' of being Machiavellian in my role as the Killer, I would say that the accusation implied I had an acute understanding of human nature.[26] And I do see everything so clearly . . . *except* when I become part of the picture, when emotion begins to cloud reason. But my reason's never been so cloudy that I'd carry a cigarette lighter.

* * *

I can't deny it. Control is important to me. I hate the possibility of accidents, of senseless events, that a horse could stumble over an embankment and land on top of your car, that someone you love could be snatched away by a sudden bolt of electricity. My work permits the illusion of control. I have strategies, schedules. My task is clearly defined, and there is little to be confused or misinterpreted. Which is as well because I can be overwhelmed by ambiguity. I am

---

25 Yuri Dobrolyubov, a school friend of Thompson, now working as a photographer in northern Italy.
26 Thompson appears to confuse his own position of authority and responsibility with that of the imaginary (Machiavellian) adviser. Hampton's Killer is not a consultant or departmental head, he *is* the maestro, the Prince. Thompson's confused attempts to relate Machiavelli to his moral outlook complements his failure to recognise his own aristocratic ambitions.

unable to read subtexts or body language or ulterior motives because I *over*-read them, see contradictory messages in every communication. Fear and desire cloud everything. Nothing unsaid is obvious to me, unambiguous to me, and I am terrified of responding to phantoms, of being lured into making an inappropriate declaration. And yet I am far too conscious of my own subtexts, and always fear that my body language will betray me, that I will give out messages that are so monstrously obvious that my desires are stripped naked, exposed for all to see on illuminated billboards high above Hampton Street.

* * *

To tell everything. How wonderful to set it all out . . . It wouldn't need to be the standard kiss-and-tell (kill-and-tell) memoir, it could be a fiction, an elaborate satire, a bizarre expressionistic construction. It would be overly simple for me to set about demolishing the Killer myths by contesting the standard assertions. Far better to ridicule the whole myth-making process by combining unbelievable truths with the most extravagant lies, so that finally the reader is left dizzied by the imagined *possibility* of truth. How wonderful it would be to perpetrate a grand hoax: to write my own unauthorised biography of the Killer. I've been allowing myself to be imprisoned by the narrowness of my thought, by the tired distinction between fiction and non-fiction. Where is the autobiography that is less preposterous than the most grotesque invention? Why not fake a journal such as this? Why not fake a book of correspondence between the Killer and some horrendous, imprisoned mass murderer? I could even prepare a fake manifesto written by an invented

119

adversary, a demented copycat killer.[27] Only by learning about lying, about deceit, about the nature of calculated untruths, can you begin to approach the truth—to realise your true self in words. I must speak to Justine about this unauthorised biography (better, *The Unauthorised Autobiography of Richard X—Killer*). Should I mention any of these literary ambitions to Christine? I wouldn't presume to trust her, but I could trust her to understand.

* * *

Always a surprising new fact to shatter your favourite illusions . . . Could it be true that Humpty Dumpty didn't actually begin his life as an egg but as an ineffective vehicle used in attacking fortresses in the English Civil War? (If television had covered The Dumpty Incident, how many times would they have replayed that fall? 'If you look closely, on the left side of your screen, you can see that he's lost it . . . *right there.*') I sometimes think that my life is the biography of Humpty Dumpty written by D.H. Lawrence: fine

---

27 In the opinion of Professor Nigel Browne, this section is the most contentious in Thompson's journal. It virtually dares the reader to interpret the journal as a hoax, or manipulative fabrication. Elliot had earlier found that Thompson's prediction of an invented adversary—anticipating the murder of Keiko Morimoto by a psychopathic copycat—was sufficient to indicate that Thompson was alert to the conspiracy to murder Morimoto, if not an active collaborator. Conversely, Witherspoon argued that a person who was capable of gaining access to Thompson's security codes could have obtained access to his journals. Thompson's privately expressed fears and speculations could have been used to manufacture a pretext that would implicate him in the murders of Morimoto and Christine Marker's film crew.

intentions and dark, dark impulses, a personality too fragile to survive in a world of violent passions.

* * *

Nearer the event, time expands and contracts all at once. I've hardly given a moment's thought to next week's speech. Once, I hoped that these speeches would amount to a kind of personal declaration, but I am so inarticulate, and whatever I propose to communicate is finally crushed by the monotony of my speaking voice. Initially, the Council asked me to speak in a way that demystified the Killer's function, but just now I feel a powerful attraction to mystique.

* * *

Is it only an insane selfishness that allows me to think of the Killer as some kind of utterly selfless dignitary?[28]

* * *

I have been invited to Buenos Aires to address an international forum on cruelty. Are the organisers being ironic? I hate the idea of cruelty. I wouldn't even wish to torture a torturer. Cruelty is superstition. It says that there is a finite amount of evil in the world, and the more evil you inflict on others, the less evil will remain to be inflicted on you. Of course, the opposite is true. Cruelty is a muscle. The magnifying

---

28 I number myself among the scholars who believe that this is the closest Thompson gets to genuine self-perception. Because of the statement's force of truth, he feels constrained to express it as mock self-deprecation.

glass you held above the unsuspecting ant as a child gave you some idea of what it would be like to be a malevolent God. But finally you were forced to concede that belief in the possibility of a truly evil God was as cruel as any cruelty you could inflict. Your earth shifts in relation to the sun, and your glass is always double-sided.

* * *

Christine, a deep red blouse to match her lips. The vibrancy of her eyes. She wants to know about the Angela Kaufmann grubbiness. This is a ruse, a subtext, surely. Under the intensity of her gaze, I feel like those ants beneath the magnifying glass, fried by a concentrated beam of light . . . I remember the humid evening I declared my love to Francesca, knowing that she would have to turn me down. Neither of us looking up, in case we caught each other's eyes. A racket of birds outside. Swallowed up by concentrated time. When I spoke to Francesca then, I felt as if I was trying to communicate with someone on a faraway star, knowing the impossibility of words being transmitted over that kind of distance. How can you appear in front of a camera, appear candid, without being seduced by the foolishness that people will hear you and understand what you mean? Why can I not just tell everything?

* * *

People are so thoughtful. In this morning's mail, a typewritten quote on a long strip of paper, a statement made by the character Luzhin in *Crime and*

Punishment (should I confess that I haven't read *Crime and Punishment*?)[29]: 'There's a limit to everything . . . An economic theory is not the equivalent to an incitement to murder.' I could hardly disagree with that, but the citizens of Hampton are no slaves to economic theory. If Hampton has a lesson to offer the world, it is that economics must be subordinate to the will to associate, that economic prosperity is the natural *biproduct* of social cohesion rather than the *route* to social cohesion. A society prospers by keeping vital the tenets of association. My anonymous correspondent should worry about dictatorial regimes who engage in 'social cleansing' for the sake of their tourist industries, about the people who have streetkids 'disappeared' by death squads so that the beaches of Rio are safe for wealthy foreigners. I'd be the first to abandon Hampton if Hampton and its Festival moved outside the control of Hampton's citizens . . .

* * *

Everything about life is incomplete, unfinished business. How many times will I have the same dream? I am at school, about to do my final examination, when

29 The copy of *Crime and Punishment* found in Thompson's bookcase was thick with marginal notes in Thompson's own hand. Either Thompson is lying about not having read the book, or he read it (and failed to note having read it) between the time of this entry and the murder of Morimoto. Testimony before the Elliot Commission argued that this omission of itself suggested a character sufficiently erratic to have been involved in the murder. Nevertheless, as Witherspoon later emphasised, Thompson did not cast himself in the role of Raskolnikov. Though he may have known of a plot to murder the prostitute Keiko Morimoto, he had an iron-clad alibi. (He was being interviewed by Christine Marker at the time of the killing.)

I discover that I am about to be examined in a subject I haven't studied all year . . . geography or mathematics. I feel powerless like this now, knowing that if I were suddenly to become sick, or incapacitated in some way, the year's plans would collapse. That's the danger of working with such small margins of error. If an intended Martyr does something spontaneous or unpredictable, forgets an appointment or an obligation, five or six months of research can go out the window. And that leads to those terrifying moments when things are out of control, when you have to make a decision on the spot, when the success of the enterprise is nothing more than an outrageous gamble. A real murderer would feel exhilaration when the gamble pays off, from getting away with it. I almost shut down with terror.

*　*　*

It's been years since I've felt such a ferocious desire to drink myself legless. I need to construct and fabricate, to insulate myself from Christine's inquisitions. Or else, I should get thoroughly tanked and confide in her, unburden myself totally. Unburden is probably the wrong word; it would be more like a Swiftian 'unburthening'—the cosmic clearout, the grand evacuation. This morning's horoscope was no help.

GEMINI In a period when you would welcome even a suggestion of what your future is to be, unfortunately you may have to endure a little longer a sense of uncertainty.

I'm being harassed by sexlessness and love-hunger,

and by a future that never seems to draw any closer. There must be someone with whom I could experience a mutuality of need and desire. If I were fully attentive, I could see her approach, *feel* her approach, backward through history. The future will reach back to caress me, to tell me, 'Here, this is Necessity, take her, you can love her, she needs you, and you alone can love her.' Does the future have this power to reach backwards, to reshape the constellations that direct love to those in need of love? I'm prattling again. Avoiding the work that needs to be done. But I want to be away from here, to be in Paris at New Year, eating crepes . . . Yes, you've heard it all before.

* * *

Sometimes at night I hear the tinkle of the old milk cart, and the clip-clopping of the milkhorse that used to round the bend of Passchendaele Street in the early hours of the morning. It's not a conscious act of imagining or remembering so much as an involuntary memory-flash. The sound is *there*. I am hearing something real. In the same way, I sometimes hear the school bell, and the sound of kids playing on the high school oval, though the school's been gone for many years now. Why is it that the old Hampton won't leave me? The rattle of coins in the big silver tin left out for the bread man (can you imagine leaving money sitting out in a public place?), the smell of the butcher shop, the floods caused by blocked stormwater drains, the neurotically neat Anglophile gardens with their gnomes, the red rattler trains with compartments divided into Smoking and No Smoking sections, the man opening the old gates at the Hampton Street level crossing, the W.C. Fields films screened at the local scout hall, and the sight of people *walking*—walking as people seldom walk now when every home must have at least two cars, and when all shopping must be done in one stop. Hampton was a meat and three veg suburb, a fish and chips on a Friday night suburb. This was Hampton long before the pizzerias and video rental shops. People asked after your mother and father, confident that you belonged to a family that they knew. They went to church on Sunday, and the religious education teachers at school could presume that all decent people did go to church on Sunday. Hampton was still full of the old people then, the Great War veterans, or their widows, who lived on the estate built for soldiers returning from the Great War: Favril Street, Amiens Street, Rouen Street, Passchendaele Street. If you drank alcohol in Hampton, you drank beer from tall brown bottles. Hampton people didn't drink wine. Very few of them could afford spirits . . . If you could have all that back again, the old Hampton, the childhood trailing behind your mother's apron strings, you probably wouldn't want it. It would all seem so unendurably dull now. Dreadfully naive. Yet it seems crucial to me that it was there, and that I am here to vouch for it, to know that there were people who cared about Hampton, people who loved it dearly for all its suburban tediousness, and that it disappeared despite their affection . . . What am I resisting? Change? Maturity? Corruption? I am a hoarder of possessions and associations and memories and momentos and scraps that say that I once inhabited a time and a world that is lost forever. As much as I might try to possess or reconstruct the past, it evaporates, little by little. What would it be to totally dispossess yourself of these emotions, to erase these scraps of meaning? Is the Killer a dispenser, or a repossessor? Or is he finally no different to anyone else, a helpless pawn of Time? . . .

* * *

If everything is predetermined, then the future will head towards you at the same speed that you head towards it, and your registration of time will be an experienced sequence of collisions that are more or less inevitable, more or less fatal.

* * *

The speech was a fiasco. An underprepared rehash of all the things I'd said a million times before. I'd intended to speak about self-sacrifice, using something that I'd heard the other day. Apparently there is an animal in northern Africa, the naked mole rat, which burrows under the ground, serving a queen (Can you imagine her pride, *I'm Queen of the Mole Rats!*), and within the mole rat community there is a special task force of these worker mole rats whose function is to sacrifice themselves if the colony is threatened. Whether this suicidal activity is behavioural or genetic doesn't really concern me, the future of naked mole rat society depends on these (occasional) acts of heroic self-sacrifice. The problem with using this in the speech is that I was still a little cloudy on how the whole thing worked, and how I could work it into my narrative without having some smartarse concluding that all the heroic self-sacrifice of Hampton's citizenry had only led to this moment where the Martyrs would be likened to naked mole rats.

* * *

A job done, without fuss or complication,[30] but I feel strange, as if I'm about to be brought undone, have the rug pulled out from under me. Maybe it's that I've just finished reading Toni Morrison's *Beloved*, and I'm full of omens, auguries, and tomorrows. This morning, I was standing over the kitchen sink, making a cup of coffee, when I looked out into the backyard and saw three ducks fly past, no more than two metres off the ground. What could it mean, a rare sighting of ducks in Hampton? An augerie, 'Three ducks at dawn, Killer be warned.'[31]

* * *

A letter from Dad today. It's rare that he comments on my role, or anything to do with the Festival, (He loathes my trade)[32] but he is adamant I should confront the Council and force them to state an attitude with regard to my proposal. He believes that the Council's failure to respond represents a threat to my autonomy, that their loyalty to me may be frail. I have tended to view their silence as a demarcation, as part of a determination to delineate powers. I have supposed that they fear the possibility of the Killer using his public profile to usurp power. Still, I have never acted disloyally in my dealings with the Council, and some response is required as a measure of their

---

30 An allusion to the killing of Marie Donkersloot on October 30.
31 The Elliot and Witherspoon Commissions spent a considerable amount of time debating the apparent over-pointedness, or sign-posting in Thompson's journal. So much of what Thompson writes seems to anticipate his fate.
32 For security reasons, the Hampton Council financed the expatriation of Thompson's immediate family. The then secret location has since been revealed to be Vancouver.

continued good faith. I didn't expect that they would immediately accept my proposal,[33] merely that it would provoke a very necessary debate on the long-term outlook for the Festival. I think Dad sees the Council chopping me off at the knees . . . Is there a subtext to all this? Maybe Dad isn't talking about the Festival at all, but using the matter to imply my treachery to my parents. Despite the material comforts of their situation, they see themselves as living in exile, cut off from their country, their friends, and their youngest son. (Could that have been my objective all along, to use the terms and conditions of the role as a necessary wedge, as an excuse not to make my peace with them? Tracey once told the press that my parents were the first casualties of the Festival, and that they deserve a place of honour in the Shrine of The Martyrs.)

* * *

Christine was on the phone this evening, and needed

---

33 According to Thompson's father, Thompson submitted a ten-page proposal that argued that the killings ought to stop after the fiftieth killing. Thompson believed that the continuing tourism and investments would be sufficient to maintain a prosperous Hampton community, and that the end of killings would free Hampton of the pressures caused by gambling as well as the boycotts imposed by external governments who disapproved of the Festival. No trace of this proposal has been found. Witherspoon argued that the Council would have seen such a proposal as a threat that Thompson would withdraw his services if they failed to comply, and feared that he might act thereafter as a subversive or oppositional force. Such an implied threat could have been sufficient to motivate a conspiracy to incriminate and/or dispose of Thompson.

to be reminded of the protocols . . .[34] I haven't mentioned that I spoke to her briefly before the speech,
while they were setting up at the back of the audito-
rium. I don't remember what we discussed, only that
she stood so close, nearly on my toes, invading my
personal space, as the Californians would say. What
should I make of this, short-sightedness or intimacy?
Her colleagues looked slightly uneasy, part of the
grand plan perhaps. I was disconcerted, yet I tried to
draw-off the warmth of her, to inhale the smell of her.
She hardly wastes a word. Her eyes touch you like the
caress of a geisha.

* * *

In red paint on the wall of the cinema, and in black
on the wall of the library, and in bill posters pasted
to construction sites and power poles:
    COMING SOON, 33 WITH A BULLET
Wendy suggests that it's a band or a new theatre work.
You have to admire their thoroughness. An unofficial
festival, a shadow Hampton, is gathering around the
official ceremonies and events. Society is always strain-
ing at the limits, testing its boundaries.

* * *

Just for the moment, things are quiet and time is mine.
I watched *The Return of Martin Guerre* on video this
afternoon. A wonderful film which details a fiction that
becomes more real, more necessary than authenticity
itself. The people need to believe in the fake Martin

---

34 According to tradition, the Killer was expected to stay out of the
   public gaze during the one week mourning period that followed
   each killing.

Guerre. Truth is an investment, and truth-seekers ride the roulette wheel of belief. *Martin Guerre* is about the process of creating a true fiction: persuasion, seduction, confrontation, believability, utility. Memories, dreams, and fantasies are like little Martin Guerres running around inside your head, and, if you heartily believe that they are real, you *make* them real, you breathe reality into them. Reality can be redefined to accommodate them . . . If I was to write a fake version of this journal, or to present this version (or a version more real than this one) as a fabricated journal, I might be able to communicate a truth that wouldn't be tainted by the weight of *the* Truth. Would Christine act as my front, as a fabricated 'ghost' writer or editor? What game could be more wildly exotic than a killer turned fabulist who imagines a (real) French novelist and maker of documentaries as the proxy author of an authentic memoir which pretends to be fake? There would be so many masks and screens and mediated meanings that the most banal observation would be impossibly loaded and reverberant. But there is the bind. Can a killer who is not a fiction writer hope to imagine how an experienced French novelist would imagine and present the day-to-day thoughts of a killer, the Killer who is contractually forbidden from writing about the very acts which make his story worth telling?

* * *

When I got back from the Council offices, the red light was flashing on my answering machine: Mary, very distressed, her voice at first unrecognisable, calling to say that Ray had been killed, stabbed to death in the

131

middle of London.[35] I couldn't get back to her, so I called her mother. Apparently they were going home after seeing a Pirandello in the West End. A vagrant approached them. Mary nodded him away, but Ray stopped to give him a coin. Suddenly he was being stabbed, no warning, a frenzy of knife blows to his chest. He died right there on the street. For nothing. People all about. They were coming back to Sydney in two weeks anyway. Mrs D. said that Mary was inconsolable. They'd set themselves up, were going to start a family soon, do all the things that they'd put on hold . . . Everything's fucked. London is totally fucked now, worse than New York, because you prepare yourself for the madness when you go to New York, you associate that kind of violent insanity with people squeezed out of the American Dream, but, I dunno, the lines of propriety have always been so clearly drawn in England, and now, when people are forced across the line, it's like all deals are off. It's as though you have to be crazy in order to make yourself visible. That's always been my worst fear for society here, the final collapse of compassionate values, the view that one class of people is expendable . . . You empty out the institutions, you pull away the safety nets, you empty the charity from people's hearts, and you have nothing but cruel hopelessness and disorder, the kind of anarchy that doesn't even respect the idea of anarchy. It's . . . I dunno. Can you restore values to a society that's abandoned every value but monetary value? The old values were only ever there to protect the interests of the privileged in the first place. How do you decide what really matters? Believe in something, anything. In God? Maybe just the possibility of

---

35 Identities unknown, possibly former teaching colleagues.

God. Something, if only the importance of believing in a thing itself and not its economic bi-product . . . Poor Ray. What will I ever be able to say that would be of any consolation to Mary?

JOURNAL ENDS

The multi-million dollar industry surrounding Hampton's Killer shows no sign of easing off. Barely a week passes without Richard Thompson being 'sighted', enjoying the high life in some remote part of the globe. Often, these sightings have Thompson in the company of a woman who resembles the film-maker Christine Marker.

In the meantime, anonymous informants describe the circumstances of Thompson and Marker's deaths. Graves where Thompson and Marker are said to be buried are exhumed. All unidentified male corpses found in Australia are presumed to be Thompson's until proven otherwise. High circulation magazines delight in featuring bizarre stories: I WAS THE PLASTIC SURGEON WHO CHANGED RICHARD THOMPSON'S FACE, and I WAS THE JUSTICE OF THE PEACE WHO MARRIED CHRISTINE TO THE KILLER.

The need for circus notwithstanding, arguments regarding the moral justification of the defunct Hampton Festival continue to rage. Though monuments dedicated to the Killer are frequently vandalised, Thompson's supporters remain loyal. Each year on June 3, large crowds gather in Hampton to celebrate Richard Thompson's birthday.

The author, Miranda Murray, argues that the absent Killer has become what the diarist Richard Thompson wanted to become, lost among the endless possible versions of himself, everything yet nothing. The Killer has come to embody a reverberant fantasy of hope and disillusionment.*

I hold a contrary view that Thompson represents nothing more than the selfish pursuit of fame at any price. Had he been a hero worthy of the heroic myth he sought to generate and promote, Thompson would have offered himself as a

---

* Murray, *If Looks Could Kill.*

sacrifice to match the sacrifices that he expected from his loyal subjects. Upon discovering the corruption of the Hampton Festival, a true Prince would have sacrificed himself to restore meaning to the heroic dedication of the Martyrs. Thompson's journals indicate that the social contract administered by the Killer was always subservient to Thompson's immediate personal agenda.

Richard Thompson desired something beyond mere authority. He craved anointment. We know that Thompson was bitterly disappointed by his failure to persuade the Council to institute an annual ceremony where the community would symbolically bequeath to the Killer his entitlement to kill. Thompson's attraction to ritual connects with his notion of a 'weird priesthood' in a more perverse way than the Killer might have imagined.

Many psychiatrists interpret Thompson's project as an Oedipal adventure. In Heather O'Donnell's monumental work, *Packing Death: Where Fear is The Killer*, the author argues that Thompson's failure to differentiate between the restored Hampton he yearns for, and the radically altered Hampton all about him, mirrors his failure to acknowledge that his crucial desire is not to restore or reconstruct the Hampton of his lost childhood, but to fashion a renovated womb: a palace of undifferentiated affection designed to celebrate the Prince's sexual fidelity to his mother, The Queen.

Hampton was Richard Thompson's Motherland in every sense of the term.

Thompson's family have been understandably reluctant to engage in discussion or analysis of the Killer's activities. They are certain that Richard was murdered as part of an attempt to obscure the criminal conspiracies operating at the heart of Hampton's Festival of Killing.

Turning their back on Hampton and its rampant commercialism, his parents erected a small memorial in the cemetery at Kerang, the country town where Richard was born. Perhaps their true feelings about their son's misadventures are expressed by the strangely ambiguous inscription:

RICHARD THOMPSON
1960–
our beloved son
missing in Utopia

APPENDICES

APPENDIX 1
THE LETTERS

On November 9, Richard Thompson received an anonymous, typewritten letter from a person who appeared to be claiming responsibility for the murder of Keiko Morimoto. Thompson immediately forwarded the letter to Inspector Nick Ptsouris. In the weeks following Richard Thompson's disappearance, the letter's author, '33 With a Bullet' emerged as the prime suspect for Hampton's spate of murders and disappearances.

The letter suggested the existence of a madman determined to compete with Hampton's Killer. Yet forensic evidence at the coronial inquest pointed in a different direction. Expert witnesses testified that the copycat murderer's letter had been produced on Richard Thompson's bubble-jet printer. The Coroner, Helen O'Brien, opined that Thompson and '33 With a Bullet' were one and the same. She argued that Thompson had fabricated a psychopathic adversary in order to conceal his own part in the conspiracy to murder Keiko Morimoto.

Though unable to identify the letter's author, Elliot and Witherspoon were reluctant to accept Thompson's involvement in its production, and stated the view that the letter was almost certainly the work of the same person, or persons, who had used Thompson's codes following Morimoto's murder.

Thompson's resignation letter of the following day did not surface for three years. In her testimony before the Coroner and Elliot, Lorraine di Stasio had denied knowledge of such a document. The discovery of the letter by a private investigator proved to be the turning point of the Witherspoon Inquiry.

Why would di Stasio have concealed the existence of the letter if she had not been determined to implicate

Thompson in order to conceal her own guilt? And, if Thompson had possessed knowledge of a conspiracy, why would he have concealed that knowledge from (a presumed co-conspirator) di Stasio? Witherspoon judged that it was likely that Thompson's letter of resignation motivated di Stasio to have Thompson silenced.

Di Stasio would later claim that she lied about the existence of the letter because the proposal to which Thompson refers had been one to involve the Council in secret gambling measures which would have freed Hampton from the need for further killings. Unable to produce Thompson's proposal, di Stasio claimed that a private investigator must have destroyed it following the break-in which uncovered Thompson's letter of resignation. No copy of the proposal Thompson put to Hampton Council has ever come to light, and speculation about the nature of Thompson's proposal continues to be fiercely debated.

MR WORTHLESS-SHIT KILLER,

Let me tell you something about passion, because what you know about passion could be written in big letters on an arrow-head. Killing's a game for a warm-blooded cunt, not for reptiles with calculators and expense accounts.

You don't know shit, Killer.

Because you don't know shit, you're not worth shit, you're just a fuckhead whose [SIC] never known the thrill of killing for killing's sake. A real killing's like a bungey-jump, you're just way out there. You don't want a soft landing. You don't want your motion to be arrested. You just want to kill again and keep killing till the rope snaps. You want to plunge hard-dicked into the crowd with one final shriek like a kamikaze's Tora Tora Tora in the face of the lynchmob, because when you're on the razor's edge, you've got to _live_ at the edge, you can't just pretend, politely disposing of decent worthwhile people when your Hampton's so full of its pimps and whores and fuck-monkeys. You don't know shit.

Sure, there [SIC] going to call me a copy-cat, because this place has no imagination, but I'm not _copying_ you, I'm not emulating you . . . I'm not a mirror held up to show you what you are and what you've done, I'm the mirror that shows you what you're _not_, I'm the mirror that reflects your miserable fucking lack of substance. Where is the Killer with blood in his veins and cum in his balls? Where is the Killer who thrives on challenge and competition? You think you're so civilised, that you're the epitome of epitomies, but this civilisation of yours is just an orchestrated surrender to death, a castrated surrender to death, a veneer to conceal everything that's venereal, the monkey-fuckers, and the monkeys who dance for the organ-grinder and all the whores who grind the organ-grinders' organs. You haven't _seen_ anything. You haven't _been_ anything. You're just vapour pretending to be a cloud. Where's your pride, Killer? It's not in your dick, that's for sure. All you are is the control that propagates control. You can't even imagine what it is to be what you should be. I'm the crisis of your imagination. It's got to be better to die in flames than live in chains. You're not worth shit, Mr Worthless-Shit Killer, and I intend to show you that you're not worth shit.

Oh my, look at this mess that you've made, a whore-girl swimming in a whore-girl's blood. You should have kept the streets clean. Now the Hampton killing monopoly is all done. The Festival of Killing is Dead. LONG LIVE THE FESTIVAL OF DEATH!!!

COMING SOON, 33 WITH A BULLET

Lorraine di Stasio
Mayor, Hampton

Dear Lorraine,

As I indicated by phone earlier today, I wish to resign from my position as of the above date. My understanding is that my contract with Hampton Council has been invalidated by the Council's failure to secure my premises, and to secure the integrity of my business dealings. Please feel free to contact my lawyer Petra Knopf at Bardons.

I'm very sorry that it has come to this. I have always performed my duties to the utmost of my abilities, and have acted in good faith with regard to the Hampton Council, and the interest of the people of Hampton. Up until the murder of Keiko Morimoto, and the violation of my private codes, I was confident that the Council was concerned with protecting my interests and the on-going prosperity of the Festival.

I have been foolish and naive. I certainly ought to have acted more firmly when the Council failed to address the proposal I submitted in June. I now see that I ought to have been concerned by the increasing number of 'non-Hampton' people elected to the Council, or in the Council's employ. And I ought to have been concerned (scared shitless even) that highly inexperienced business managers would lack the capacity to handle a festival that had grown far beyond our wildest hopes.

I am hurt and confused. Why am I now so inclined to believe in rumours, even the far-fetched (?) rumours: that the Council has been infiltrated by, or is working in cahoots with, foreign intelligence agencies, and that the Council has been acting as an intermediary in arms deals? I also have a strong suspicion that this '33 With a Bullet' character is a fabrication, a psychopath of convenience. Whose interests would such a fabrication serve? How could a person so apparently erratic gain access to the codes and channels without drawing attention

145

to his activities? And why was the 'Coming Soon, 33 With a Bullet' graffiti allowed to linger on the walls of public buildings? (The Council has always made a big issue out of cleaning graffiti upon discovery.) This man has been *allowed* to be very conspicuously conspicuous.

I want no part in murderous challenges. I have lost the desire to carry out the Killer's duties, and I have lost confidence in the role of the Killer. I am now of the opinion that the Festival has been irreparably corrupted.

To begin with, I firmly believed that the Festival would restore the former Hampton, a place where people knew each other, and cared about the future of the community. What's more, that Hampton would be restored as a place where community was considered to be valuable in itself. I always thought that the gambling was intended to act as a cushion until tourism was firmly established, rather than the monstrous be all and end all it has become.

If my only concern was that everyone was not pulling in the same direction, I'd be the first to initiate a recommitment to the Festival and what it was intended to stand for. I now doubt that it was ever possible for everyone to pull in the same direction. There was an inevitability about this Morimoto tragedy.

While acting as the Killer, I have always lived under threat, so I am not unaware that I place myself in further jeopardy by resigning at this time. I trust that you will respect my reasons and accept my resignation in good faith.

Yours sincerely,

rt.

Richard Thompson

Crucial documents related to Hampton's Festival still continue to surface at regular intervals.

This volume was just about to be sent to the printers when a previously unexamined letter sent by Christine Marker to her sister Isabelle in Montparnasse was 'discovered'.

Scholars were alerted to the existence of this letter when Isabelle Marker, a journalist, requested its return following the final report of the Witherspoon Commission. As it transpired, neither Elliot nor Witherspoon had considered the document. The letter, written in French and untranslated, had been mislaid among papers forwarded to the original coronial inquest.

Christine Marker's letter gives us a particularly intimate view of her feelings about Richard Thompson and the Hampton Festival, and it appears to settle the question of whether Marker might have (willingly) absconded with Hampton's Killer. Her letter also suggests that the central concern of Marker's documentary would have been to connect Hampton's Festival with dominant cultural trends in Australian/Western capitalist society.

The translation which appears here has been provided by Miranda Murray.

November 4

My Very Dear Isabelle,

I'm so sorry, I should have written long before this. Your wonderful
letter arrived three weeks ago. I could pretend that work has got the
better of me, but time is a concertina here, it opens and folds according
to need. The truth is that my time has been much more occupied with
the thought of work than the actual demands of work . . .

[Two pages have been omitted at the request of Isabelle Marker,
where Christine comments on personal matters raised in Isabelle's
letter.]

. . . I am beginning to get some idea of the shape that the film might
take. Certain themes recur and intersect. Before we came to Hampton,
I thought that so much of the Festival—the possibility of rationalising
a killing spree such as this—must hinge on the Killer's personality.
Now I find my position shifting. The Killer, though he is a fascinating
case, is no anomaly or psychiatric phenomenon. He's the insecure
product of an insecure society. Richard Thompson is a passionless
man who wants to represent himself as an archetypal Australian hero,
the lone surfer riding a wave of social redefinition. He needs to keep
reiterating his position in order to maintain belief in it. But the Killer
is far from alone in his emotional frailty. Intellectual life is so
marginalised here that intellectuals habitually take defensive positions
and refuse themselves the vulnerability of passion. When these meek
intellectuals finally begin to toy with fire, they have no intuition for
the dangers of misdirected passion.

Thompson is like an Australian Godzilla. Kind, half-apologetic, a
powerhouse of good intentions, but at every turn he crushes a building
or brings down a powerline or tramples a schoolbus . . . Or King
Kong. (I may have become Fay Wray to his King Kong.) He's
attracted to me, but he's far too gormless to act on his attraction. The
rest of the crew find it ridiculous, with the Killer trying so hard to
be decent and impressive, to represent himself as a serious-minded
socio-political theorist. Michael wants me to seduce him. He thinks
that a Mata Hari might have him expose the underside of his personality. I find him intriguing but totally undesirable. Too short, too

148

indefinite. I can't imagine wanting to kiss a man with such bulbous gums. He still puzzles me. How can an obviously intelligent man become so removed from his emotions that he is able to divorce himself from the horror of his responsibility for the murders? (The word murder is a taboo here.)

Thompson persists in arguing that his interest is community, that he is a knight trying to defend the threatened values of community. I suspect that the opposite is closer to the truth. I think that he so deeply laments the way that Hampton changed in the years prior to the Festival, the loss of everything associated with the community he grew up in, that he is now acting to speed the destruction of the festively avaricious Hampton, this new Babylon. By accelerating Hampton's destruction, he hopes to retrieve his lost childhood. He hopes to salvage and restore the sanctity of his memories of a Hampton childhood. In this respect, Thompson is less the disinterested agent carrying out official policy than he is a rogue *Catcher in the Rye* figure—Holden Caulfield with a crossbow. The Killer imagines that he is trying to save people from Life's failure to honour its promise of possible ecstasy, and he extrapolates a sense of purpose and worth from his own disillusionment.

The Killer is far from alone in this. His exaggerated disillusionment and sense of failure seem to be typical of a culture which defines itself by its failure to realise American dreams, by its inability to replicate an impossible Hollywood version of American reality.

And neither are his victims the selfless heroes that they make themselves out to be. Hampton's martyrs are not the Burghers of Calais, surrendering themselves to the enemy in the hope of ending an interminable siege. What Mark Twain once said is true, 'Martyrdom covers a multitude of sins'. So many of the Hampton people that I speak to express a fervrent desire to be martyred. But very few of them impress as people who are determined to enrich their community through altruistic sacrifice. They must see martyrdom as a release. It promises to release them from their habitual greed, from the guilty knowledge that they have grown fat gorging on the flesh of their martyred neighbours. The wealth they have—a very material wealth—is born out of cannibalism. And it's not only the martyrs who are devoured. Most analysts neglect the anonymous victims of related exploitation, the children of the gambling-addicted and the commercially obsessed. So much in Australia centres on sports and gambling and alcohol, and there are some very perverse understandings of what truly noble action involves.

Hampton is no paradise. It's comfortable in its tastelessness. If Los Vegas represents Hell on Earth, Hampton is an antechamber en route to Purgatory. There is always activity, but what excitement or buzz there is here is so artificial. Dollar-driven cynicism motivates everything related to the Festival. The real joy is to escape from Hampton, to escape Melbourne. You need to get right out of the city, two or three hours away, down to the southern ocean where a spectacular road winds along sheer cliffs. With Hampton caught up in its mourning rituals, Michael rented a zippy Japanese sedan, and we escaped for the weekend, taking our wine and picnic to Apollo Bay. Apollo Bay is a magnificent crescent of white sand surrounded by steep green hills. A small Heaven, a million kilometres from Hampton's neon hyperbole. The quiet coastal villages with their fabulous beaches are symbols of the egalitarianism that Australians habitually venerate, but turn their back on in practice: a simple richness of existence that excludes no one. And that's it, precisely. Anything that doesn't exclude is worthless. If something can't be sold and packaged by advertising agencies, if it can't be commodified, it can't have value.

It was unseasonably warm at the coast. The sand was fine and hot under our feet, and it was like being a kid again. We volleyed Gillian's beachball, drank wine, stuffed ourselves with chicken and salads, and waved away flies and mosquitos, all feeling so famously anonymous behind our sunglasses. The water was still too cold to swim, but the sun was hot, the air thick and moist. Penny soon became a lobster in her enthusiasm to tan. Children shrieked as they ran between the sand dunes, fishing boats bobbed about on the horizon, and wisps of breeze fluttered off the ocean. Perfect. We stayed at a guesthouse in the hills, and woke to the sound of birds: magpies, parrots, and currawongs. And then an awesome electrical storm with breakfast that soon gave way to a clear, cool day.

I would've chosen anything but to drive back to Melbourne then. To spend a month walking the hills and forests and beaches. But I was happy too to feel the wind through the open window, to sing along like teenagers to the old songs on Michael's tape: Talking Heads, The The, The Smiths. On the western fringe of the city, a huge bridge, the West Gate, curves through the sky above the Maribyrnong River. You see the orange of the setting sun reflect off the glass towers that make up central Melbourne, and you can look out across the water towards Hampton to the south-east. I aimed my video-camera at the sky above Hampton then, hoping against hope that a flaming Killer would choose that moment to tumble from the heavens and plummet into the bay.

Some dreams are more likely to be realised than others. I still hope to see you in Strasbourg—*with Henri*—at Christmas. You mustn't be too hard on Henri. He's just a man, and I've seen many worse men. Selfish as Henri is, he would at least know the difference between self-interest and nobility. Take care, my darling.

All My Love,

C.

APPENDIX 2
THE HAMPTON MARTYRS

In April this year, after prolonged public debate, a decision was made to represent Keiko Morimoto, Penny Donaldson, Gillian Chatterton, Michael Tynan, and Christine Marker in the main gallery of Hampton's Shrine of The Martyrs. As yet, no agreement has been reached on the proposal to represent Richard Thompson in the Shrine.

YEAR 1

1   **CATHY SINCLAIR 28**, unmarried, teacher, crossbow
2   **DAVIS SUMP 67**, unmarried, invalid pensioner, lethal injection
3   **NICK ERMANOS 25**, married, father of one, bank teller, lethal injection
4   **CHRISTINE NELSON 44**, married, mother of six, shop assistant, crossbow
5   **NOEL TARPEY 54**, married, father of four, casino manager, drowned
6   **FRANK HAJNCL 37**, married, father of two, sports administrator, poisoned
7   **DESPINA MERLOT 17**, unmarried, student, poisoned

YEAR 2

8   **MICHAEL BENSON 23**, unmarried, manager of the band Approximate Life, hanged

9 & 10 **TRAN AND JESSICA NGUYEN 36 and 33,** parents of two, hotel managers, poisoned

11 **MARGARET FARRELLY 49,** unmarried, dental technician, drowned

12 **CONRAD MITCHELL 44,** married, father of three, greengrocer, fed to sharks

13 **DAVID MILLER 28,** unmarried, solicitor, crossbow

14 **PETER METHERALL 64,** unmarried, manager of construction company, crossbow

YEAR 3

15 **JOHNNY BILLINGSLEY 40,** divorced, father of two, local government administrator, poisoned

16 **GAIL WILLIAMS 39,** married, mother of five, gift shop manager, smothered

17 **CAROL MIFSUD 48,** divorced, mother of two, architect, lethal injection

18 **KAREN PETERSON 31,** unmarried, public relations consultant, electrocuted

19 **ROBERT ADAMS 38,** unmarried, writer/composer, hanged

20 **ANGELA KAUFMANN 15,** unmarried, student, smothered

21 **GUNTER FASSBINDER 86,** widowed, father of six, retired magician, smothered

YEAR 4

22 **BERYL CHUNG 53,** married, mother of three, librarian, cause of death unknown

23 **AMBROSE TATE** 16, unmarried, student, pushed from roof
24 **CLIFF TULSE** 29, divorced, no children, circus performer, sabotaged trapeze
25 **SANDY OLUFSEN** 19, unmarried, university student, drowned
26 **LEONIE RICHARDSON** 61, unmarried, school principal, lethal injection
27 **SAM PASQUALIDIS** 46, unmarried, father of two, bottle shop manager, pushed from cliff
28 **COLLEEN FENELEY** 53, widowed, mother of six, hair dresser, crossbow

YEAR 5

29 **JACK GODDARD** 59, divorced, father of two, builder, lethal injection
30 **FRANCES KING** 52, married, mother of three, real estate agent, crossbow
31 **JULIE AHMAD** 25, unmarried, mother of one, designer, smothered
32 **JIM FITZGERALD** 58, unmarried, artist, crossbow
33 **MARTIN O'BRIEN** 33, unmarried, importer, lethal injection
34 **MARIE DONKERSLOOT** 41, married, mother of two, general practitioner, crossbow

ALSO

KEIKO MORIMOTO 23, unmarried, exotic dancer, murdered

PENNY DONALDSON 34, unmarried, sound technician, murdered

MICHAEL TYNAN 43, married, father of two, cameraman, murdered

GILLIAN CHATTERTON 24, divorced, no children, researcher, murdered

CHRISTINE MARKER 35, unmarried, author/filmmaker, presumed murdered